John Wilson

in search of Dreams

Morteza Kamali

Title: John Wilson in search of Dreams
Author: Morteza Kamali
Editor: Ms. Elahe Vahidi
Cover designer Hasan Ebrahimi
Publisher: Supreme Art, USA
ISBN: 9781942912569

Table of Content

Chapter One

Trying Survive

In the extreme cold of winter, when the steam of every breath froze in the mouth and fell to the ground, John walked down the street, rummaging around the street and trash cans to find a piece of bread. John was only thirteen years old. He was eleven years old when he lost his parents in a bank robbery; He had neither brother nor sister. After his parents were killed, the government gave his custody to his grandmother, but unfortunately, his grandmother died a few months later, and because his family was poor, they left him nothing to make a living. After his grandmother died, the government sent him to the Kingsley Orphanage, but he did not stand it and decided to flee, and finally, on a cold winter night, he carried out his decision and fled.

The first few nights were very hard; Because John was not accustomed to sleeping under stairs, parks, and next to vermin and tedious rats. When he had a family, although they were poor, they had at least a shelter to spend the night there. John decided to work for a living, but wherever he went, he was not hired because of his young age and his lean and skinny body; After all, they did not accept him when they realized that he had no family.

The night was colder than ever. The news announced the cold was unprecedented in the last 20 years. John did not have many clothes; He knew very well that if things went this way, he would not survive long; On another hand, he did not want to come back to that orphanage; because the orphanage owner was a grumpy person with a scary face named Blake. The orphanage children were silent when they saw Mr. Blake; Mr. Blake's face was so frightening that even the orphanage staff was afraid of him and they stood in awe of him. Likewise, those who worked in the orphanage did not treat the children well and sometimes servitudes them and forced them to do the work of the orphanage.

One day a terrible dispute took place between John and an employee named Mrs. Johnson. The reason for this dispute was the forced labor that was imposed on the children of the orphanage. For this reason, John no longer wanted to come back to the orphanage and was willing to endure this hardship.

John wandered down Brown Street looking for food; It was about eleven o'clock at night; There was almost no one on the street. John saw children of the same age behind the window, getting ready to go to bed, and their mother says good night to them while kissing them. Seeing these scenes, his heart ached and a teardrop warmed his face and he continued on his way until he reached a dead-end alley. At the end of the alley, there was a dumpster; John did not want to go to the dumpster, but a power forced him to do so. He walked slowly; there was a fear in his heart that would not let go, but the feeling of hunger dragged him to the dumpster so that he might find something to eat. He reached the dumpster and began to search, but he did not find anything ... After a bit of searching, he found a slice of pizza and began to eat it eagerly; and he thanked God that he had found the food to eat. He was searching again when suddenly his hand hit a hard object ... he became curious! What was so rigid! It was a mysterious place, and everything he saw or felt was special. John wanted to take out that hard object, but his hand did not reach it; He decided to turn the dumpster upside down to pick up the object, but he could not do anything because the dumpster was chained to a pole next to it.

John thought that to be able to take the object out of the dumpster, there was only one way to get into the dumpster, but it was too high for John ... After turning around a bit, his eyes fell on the wooden box; He put the box next to the dumpster and put his feet on the box, and with difficulty, he reached the top of the dumpster and threw himself into the dumpster, but when he jumped into it as if he had fallen into a deep valley, as he went deeper he did not go to the bottom of the dumpster; Finally, after a moment, his body touched the bottom of the dumpster.

John closed his eyes in fear when he was thrown down the dumpster, and when he reached the bottom, he opened his eyes and was confronted with a strange sight! It was as if John had fallen into another world; A world darker than he imagined. After some reflection, John looked for the hard object, and in the same darkness, he dragged his hand to the bottom of the dumpster until it appeared. When he saw it, it seemed nothing special, and he regretted wasting his time finding it. He dropped the object and wanted it to come out, but he looked at the black object again; He said to himself, "Well, I will take this; there is no harm." He reached out to grab the edge of the dumpster, but his hand did not reach the edge of it. His efforts were in vain and he slept there until morning.

John opened his eyes and found himself in the middle of a pile of trash. The sound of moving cars woke John; he got up and shook himself; He just remembered what happened last night and where he is now! To get out of the dumpster, he was looking for something to put under his feet. After searching, he found the black object and put it in his pocket. Finally, after searching, he found something to come up and reach the edge of the dumpster; He pulled himself up with difficulty and jumped to the other side of the dumpster, and fell on the cold street. He got up and once again remembered that alley and began to walk on the snow of the street.

John reached the stairs of a shop and wanted to sit there for a while, but the owner of the shop refused to let him sit; John also had to continue on his way, while walking he remembered the black object and decided to see the mysterious object in a secluded place, what was that hard object that drew him to itself that night?

A little further on, in a secluded alley, somewhere on the ground which has a shelter above his head, which was not covered with snow, he sat on the ground and took the object out of his pocket and examined it carefully ... The black object was like glass; A little more careful; Something was engraved on a part of that object; "John Wilson" read that text with difficulty!

John threw the black object into a corner in horror; it was his name and surname that was engraved on it! What could be the object whose name was engraved on it! And it was in the dumpster too!

After a short while he got better, he went back to that object ... After much searching, it appeared; it was covered in snow and it was a little difficult to find. He looked at the engravement again more closely; It was nothing but "John Wilson" on it!...

After some thought, John concluded that John Wilson on the object does not have to mean John himself; Maybe someone else has the same name as him! Little by little he was convinced ... he picked up the object again and looked carefully; He touched the back of the hard object; there was a metal object behind it! John looked at it very carefully to see if there was anything behind it ... Yes; it was as if there was a lock behind that glass object! He struggled with the lock and was able to unlock it. Inside was a piece of paper; He picked up the paper and looked around; No one was around to see John. As he opened the paper, a small photo fell out of the paper; John took that photo and when he saw that photo, he shouted briefly and covered his mouth with his hand ... That photo was his photo!

John was both surprised and very scared; He took the photo and looked at it; It was a photo of John at five years old!

With the sweet smile, he gave to the photographer. John noticed that part of the photo had been cut with scissors and only part of one hand remained. John put the photo in his pocket and opened the sheet of paper; It was a letter written in French, not English.

At first, he decided to give the letter to someone to translate for him, but then he thought to himself that it might be dangerous! If there is anything in that letter that benefits John, no one should know. He took the photo again and looked; This time he looked more closely at the photo; There was a picture in the photo that was fuzzy and far, but John was more careful; His curiosity was aroused. He looked at the photo very carefully; He saw something stranger ... In that picture, five-year-old John was with another man and woman; He was in the arms of a twenty-seven or eight-year-old woman with blonde hair and a flowered shirt. Her hair was combed to one side very neatly and she had a beautiful smile on her face; As if that day was the happiest day of her life. The man sitting next to the woman was in a light brown suit with eyes like John's eyes and a long nose like John's nose ... The man had a mustache and a smiling face that was full of hope.

The deeper John looked at the photo, the more he realized the similarity between himself and the man and woman. He asked why he has a photo with these people and who they are! His mind was full of various puzzles.

He looked at the back of the photo; something was written on it. The name of the place; was "France, Villa House", but the address was incomplete due to the torn photo. John sighed loudly that why the photo was half full, and on the other hand, he was happy to find a clue.

The weather was very cold, and John thought neither of hunger nor of cold; a strange force had overtaken him; He was feeling as if he wanted to turn the world upside down to solve this puzzle. His mind was full of question marks; He said to himself that there must have been a reason why I was drawn there; I have to solve this problem.

Although John was young, because of his hard life, he understood more than his age and did things that were older than his age; that's why he could analyze things so well. John had good mental strength; He was the smartest student in the class when he went to school and always answered questions the fastest; He had a curious mind and was always looking for new things.

Suddenly he came out of his thoughts; it was dark; He had been sitting there for hours, thinking about the photo; He had just realized how hungry he was. He put the letter and photo in its place; He put the black object in his pocket and got up and set off to find food and a place to sleep...

After a short walk and looking around the dumpster, he was almost slumping when he suddenly thought of the dead-end alley. John was sure he would find something to eat there. He reached the same alley; A strange and mysterious feeling came to him again; He was a little scared, but with the will and courage that the black object had given him, he stepped forward. It was covered with snow everywhere. It was snowing heavily; So the footprints do not remain for more than a few minutes. John was amazed at the force that kept him alive and could still walk and think; even, after 24 hours of starving!

He approached the dumpster; Last night's box was still there; It was as if no one was there. As he approached the dumpster, John wished there will be delicious food inside; for example, a piece of chicken that can feed himself. This time, John decided to go inside the trash from the beginning and look for food. With the cold weather, John preferred to warm himself with the rubbish in the dumpster.

He went back on the box and stepped into the world of the dumpster, and the same thing as the night before happened. With his eyes closed, John felt himself fall into a deep valley. When he reached the bottom of the dumpster, he thought of food, how to find food in this darkness among all this garbage! But despite the garbage, not only it did not smell bad, but it also smelled good. It smelled like chicken. He pushed himself closer to the food until he finally reached it ... there was a closed container there. When he opened it and saw the inside of the container, his eyes widened in surprise. He could not believe what he saw! That's what he wanted! A delicious piece of chicken with the gravy still on the chicken; It was as if someone had bought it, but did not want to eat it and threw it in the dumpster. John eagerly began to eat the chicken. That night, after a long time, John ate a good and full meal. After he was full, a deep sleep overtook his eyes and he fell asleep slowly.

He woke up again in the morning to the sound of cars. He rubbed his eyes and reconsidered what had happened last night. He was concluding that this was a special place for him, and he thanked God for His grace. He said to himself that there is a reason for all this and I have to find the reason. Surely this place and this thing want to make me realize something! I will not give up until I realize this.

The snow had stopped; there was a gentle breeze, and after hitting the snow on the street, it was cold. The wind was blowing inside the dead-end alley, making a terrible noise. Sometimes the clouds blocked out the sun in the middle of the sky. Sometimes someone would cross the alley but pass unnoticed into the alley. The children were playing in the snow. It was the Christmas holidays; many were traveling and others were playing and having fun.

John had made his decision; He thought about what he needed to do to achieve his goal. He said to himself, "Well, first of all, I have to make money and I have to find a job to make money ... but with this appearance no one hires me; they think that I am a thief. First, I have to think about my appearance." John wanted to learn French so that he could read the text of the letter himself. He decided to work first and earn money so that he could go to a French class with that money.

That day, he searched so that he might find a job, but he was rejected as soon as they saw his appearance, but John did not give up with the will he had. It was getting dark; John decided to return to his safe place; so, he took the way to the dead-end alley. He felt the same again! But this time he was not afraid at all, and on the contrary, he felt good; Sense of security; it was as if the dumpster was his home.

On the way to the dead-end alley, he thought about how good it would be if he could find the right clothes that he could use to sort himself out so that he might be able to find a good job. It was with these thoughts that he reached the alley and entered the dumpster in the same way. This time John did not wish for any special food, but he hoped in his heart that this time too God would help him and find good food. He smelled again ... he smelled good. After a bit of searching, he found food and he was happy; again, a piece of chicken in the dish with the same gravy on the chicken had fallen into the dumpster. He ate the chicken happily and thanked God for paying attention to him.

John fell asleep thinking, and woke up in the morning, as usual, to the sound of cars. As he rubbed his eyes, his eyes suddenly fell on a piece of clothing that had fallen into the dumpster. He was about to scream in astonishment; john believed that this dumpster was the bucket of wishes. John changed his clothes there, and he happily came out of the wish bucket and was happy that he could ask for money from the wish bucket tonight there was no need to work and walked the streets again, but This time he was walking the streets not to find work and food, but to explore the city ... and he felt that this time he was walking in the streets like a gentleman.

Although he did not eat anything from morning to night, it seemed that the amount of energy that the food in the trash had given him, he could spend until night very easily and not feel hungry...

It was getting dark, and John, who had come out of the dumpster in the morning, was just thinking of a bag full of money that he would find in the bucket tonight and all his problems would be solved. He was happily moving towards the dumpster, and this time, when he reached that alley, that feeling was no longer there and there was no mysterious feeling; He felt that he was no longer familiar with it. He went to the dumpster and climbed out of the box and threw himself into the dumpster, but this time he hit the bottom of the dumpster very quickly and felt severe pain! John said to him, "It must have happened because I opened my eyes!" I have to close my eyes. John was waiting for money and food and started smelling; but there was nothing, and instead of the good smell of food, he could smell the bad smell of garbage.

John did not find any food; He said to himself, "Certainly, because I did not wish what food should be in the dumpster, there is nothing here!" Then he thought, "Well, I had not wished the night before! Maybe every wish lasts only two nights!" Because his thought was more involved with money, he looked for money and said to himself, I can buy better food tomorrow and eat full with the money I find, but the more he searched, the more disappointed he became ...

He got tired after an hour of searching. He thought, "I certainly did not wish correctly that I did not find the money there" and decided to sleep there. That night, the smell of garbage bothered him a lot, but he had to sleep with that smell.

He woke up in the morning and went to the streets very hungry. He had to find something to feed. With a lot of trouble, he could find a piece of dry bread to at least get rid of that state of hunger. He thought about the money again, and this time he wished with more energy maybe the money was in the trash. Night came and John returned to that alley; without fear, he went to the dumpster and threw himself into it, and the dumpster smelled worse than the night before! Although he had closed his eyes, he felt more pain from hitting the bottom of the trash and soon reached the bottom of it. He felt that his hand was injured, but he got up and looked for money, regardless of the wound on his hand; Even food was no longer important to him; He was just looking for money, but it was in vain ... He stopped trying and the bad smell of the dumpster was no longer tolerable; He came out of the dumpster and sat and thought in a corner of the dead-end alley. That the dumpster had lost its magical power? Or there was no magic power at all and it was all an illusion or it was just a normal event!

It was in these thoughts that an idea suddenly came to his mind; He thought about what had happened; He concluded that the magic power of the dumpster had disappeared since the thought of making money effortlessly came to his mind. John found a place to sleep and was able to sleep for a few hours with all the cold and hunger. The next morning, John woke up and decided to go back and find a job. He went to the park, washed his hands and face, brushed his hair, and moved. After going to a few places, he arrived at a French restaurant.

In the extreme cold of winter, when the steam of every breath froze in the mouth and fell to the ground, John walked down the street, rummaging around the street and trash cans to find a piece of bread. John was only thirteen years old. He was eleven years old when he lost his parents in a bank robbery; He had neither brother nor sister. After his parents were killed, the government gave his custody to his grandmother, but unfortunately, his grandmother died a few months later, and because his family was poor, they left him nothing to make a living. After his grandmother died, the government sent him to the Kingsley Orphanage, but he did not stand it and decided to flee, and finally, on a cold winter night, he carried out his decision and fled.

The first few nights were very hard; Because John was not accustomed to sleeping under stairs, parks, and next to vermin and tedious rats. When he had a family, although they were poor, they had at least a shelter to spend the night there. John decided to work for a living, but wherever he went, he was not hired because of his young age and his lean and skinny body; After all, they did not accept him when they realized that he had no family.

The night was colder than ever. The news announced the cold was unprecedented in the last 20 years. John did not have many clothes; He knew very well that if things went this way, he would not survive long; On the other hands, he did not want to come back to that orphanage; because the orphanage owner was a grumpy person with a scary face named Blake. The orphanage children were silent when they saw Mr. Blake; Mr. Blake's face was so frightening that even the orphanage staff was afraid of him and they stood in awe of him. Likewise, those who worked in the orphanage did not treat the children well and sometimes servitudes them and forced them to do the work of the orphanage.

One day a terrible dispute took place between John and an employee named Mrs. Johnson. The reason for this dispute was the forced labor that was imposed on the children of the orphanage. For this reason, John no longer wanted to come back to the orphanage and was willing to endure this hardship.

John wandered down Brown Street looking for food; it was about eleven o'clock at night; there was almost no one on the street. John saw children of the same age behind the window, getting ready to go to bed, and their mother says good night to them while kissing them. Seeing these scenes, his heart ached and a teardrop warmed his face and he continued on his way until he reached a dead-end alley. At the end of the alley, there was a dumpster; John did not want to go to the dumpster, but a power forced him to do so. He walked slowly; there was a fear in his heart that would not let go, but the feeling of hunger dragged him to the dumpster so that he might find something to eat. He reached the dumpster and began to search, but he did not find anything ... After a bit of searching, he found a slice of pizza and began to eat it eagerly; and he thanked God that he had found the food to eat. He was searching again when suddenly his hand hit a hard object ... he became curious! What was so rigid! It was a mysterious place, and everything he saw or felt was special. John wanted to take out that hard object, but his hand did not reach it; He decided to turn the dumpster upside down to pick up the object, but he could not do anything because the dumpster was chained to a pole next to it.

John thought that to be able to take the object out of the dumpster, there was only one way to get into the dumpster, but it was too high for John ... After turning around a bit, his eyes fell on the wooden box; He put the box next to the dumpster and put his feet on the box, and with difficulty, he reached the top of the dumpster and threw himself into the dumpster, but when he jumped into it as if he had fallen into a deep valley, as he went deeper he did not go to the bottom of the dumpster; Finally, after a moment, his body touched the bottom of the dumpster.

John closed his eyes in fear when he was thrown down the dumpster, and when he reached the bottom, he opened his eyes and was confronted with a strange sight! It was as if John had fallen into another world; A world darker than he imagined. After some reflection, John looked for the hard object, and in the same darkness, he dragged his hand to the bottom of the dumpster until it appeared. When he saw it, it seemed nothing special, and he regretted wasting his time finding it. He dropped the object and wanted it to come out, but he looked at the black object again; He said to himself, "Well, I will take this; there is no harm." He reached out to grab the edge of the dumpster, but his hand did not reach the edge of it. His efforts were in vain and he slept there until morning.

John opened his eyes and found himself in the middle of a pile of trash. The sound of moving cars woke John; he got up and shook himself; He just remembered what happened last night and where he is now! To get out of the dumpster, he was looking for something to put under his feet. After searching, he found the black object and put it in his pocket. Finally, after searching, he found something to come up and reach the edge of the dumpster; He pulled himself up with difficulty and jumped to the other side of the dumpster, and fell on the cold street. He got up and once again remembered that alley and began to walk on the snow of the street.

John reached the stairs of a shop and wanted to sit there for a while, but the owner of the shop refused to let him sit; John also had to continue on his way, while walking he remembered the black object and decided to see the mysterious object in a secluded place, what was that hard object that drew him to itself that night?

A little further on, in a secluded alley, somewhere on the ground which has a shelter above his head, which was not covered with snow, he sat on the ground and took the object out of his pocket and examined it carefully ... The black object was like glass; A little more careful; Something was engraved on a part of that object; "John Wilson" read that text with difficulty!

John threw the black object into a corner in horror; it was his name and surname that was engraved on it! What could be the object whose name was engraved on it! And it was in the dumpster too!

After a short while he got better, he went back to that object ... After much searching, it appeared; it was covered in snow and it was a little difficult to find. He looked at the engravement again more closely; It was nothing but "John Wilson" on it!...

After some thought, John concluded that John Wilson on the object does not have to mean John himself; Maybe someone else has the same name as him! Little by little he was convinced ... he picked up the object again and looked carefully; He touched the back of the hard object; there was a metal object behind it! John looked at it very carefully to see if there was anything behind it ... Yes; it was as if there was a lock behind that glass object! He struggled with the lock and was able to unlock it. Inside was a piece of paper; He picked up the paper and looked around; No one was around to see John. As he opened the paper, a small photo fell out of the paper; John took that photo and when he saw that photo, he shouted briefly and covered his mouth with his hand ... That photo was his photo!

John was both surprised and very scared; He took the photo and looked at it; It was a photo of John at five years old! With the sweet smile, he gave to the photographer. John noticed that part of the photo had been cut with scissors and only part of one hand remained. John put the photo in his pocket and opened the sheet of paper; It was a letter written in French, not English.

At first, he decided to give the letter to someone to translate for him, but then he thought to himself that it might be dangerous! If there is anything in that letter that benefits John, no one should know. He took the photo again and looked; this time he looked more closely at the photo; there was a picture in the photo that was fuzzy and far, but John was more careful; His curiosity was aroused. He looked at the photo very carefully; He saw something stranger ... In that picture, five-year-old John was with another man and woman; He was in the arms of a twenty-seven or eight-year-old woman with blonde hair and a flowered shirt. Her hair was combed to one side very neatly and she had a beautiful smile on her face; As if that day was the happiest day of her life. The man sitting next to the woman was in a light brown suit with eyes like John's eyes and a long nose like John's nose ... The man had a mustache and a smiling face that was full of hope.

The deeper John looked at the photo, the more he realized the similarity between himself and the man and woman. He asked why he has a photo with these people and who they are! His mind was full of various puzzles.

He looked at the back of the photo; something was written on it. The name of the place; was "France, Villa House", but the address was incomplete due to the torn photo. John sighed loudly that why the photo was half full, and on the other hand, he was happy to find a clue.

The weather was very cold, and John thought neither of hunger nor of cold; A strange force had overtaken him; He was feeling as if he wanted to turn the world upside down to solve this puzzle. His mind was full of question marks; He said to himself that there must have been a reason why I was drawn there; I have to solve this problem.

Although John was young, because of his hard life, he understood more than his age and did things that were older than his age; that's why he could analyze things so well. John had good mental strength; He was the smartest student in the class when he went to school and always answered questions the fastest; He had a curious mind and was always looking for new things.

Suddenly he came out of his thoughts; it was dark; He had been sitting there for hours, thinking about the photo; He had just realized how hungry he was. He put the letter and photo in its place; He put the black object in his pocket and got up and set off to find food and a place to sleep...

After a short walk and looking around the dumpster, he was almost slumping when he suddenly thought of the dead-end alley. John was sure he would find something to eat there. He reached the same alley; a strange and mysterious feeling came to him again; He was a little scared, but with the will and courage that the black object had given him, he stepped forward. It was covered with snow everywhere. It was snowing heavily; So the footprints do not remain for more than a few minutes. John was amazed at the force that kept him alive and could still walk and think; even, after 24 hours of starving!

He approached the dumpster; Last night's box was still there; it was as if no one was there. As he approached the dumpster, John wished there will be delicious food inside; For example, a piece of chicken that can feed himself. This time, John decided to go inside the trash from the beginning and look for food. With the cold weather, John preferred to warm himself with the rubbish in the dumpster.

He went back on the box and stepped into the world of the dumpster, and the same thing as the night before happened. With his eyes closed, John felt himself fall into a deep valley. When he reached the bottom of the dumpster, he thought of food, how to find food in this darkness among all this garbage! But despite the garbage, not only it did not smell bad, but it also smelled good. It smelled like chicken. He pushed himself closer to the food until he finally reached it ... there was a closed container there. When he opened it and saw the inside of the container, his eyes widened in surprise. He could not believe what he saw! That's what he wanted! A delicious piece of chicken with the gravy still on the chicken; It was as if someone had bought it, but did not want to eat it and threw it in the dumpster. John eagerly began to eat the chicken. That night, after a long time, John ate a good and full meal. After he was full, a deep sleep overtook his eyes and he fell asleep slowly.

He woke up again in the morning to the sound of cars. He rubbed his eyes and reconsidered what had happened last night. He was concluding that this was a special place for him, and he thanked God for His grace. He said to himself that there is a reason for all this and I have to find the reason. Surely this place and this thing want to make me realize something! I will not give up until I realize this.

The snow had stopped; there was a gentle breeze, and after hitting the snow on the street, it was cold. The wind was blowing inside the dead-end alley, making a terrible noise. Sometimes the clouds blocked out the sun in the middle of the sky. Sometimes someone would cross the alley but pass unnoticed into the alley. The children were playing in the snow. It was the Christmas holidays; many were traveling and others were playing and having fun.

John had made his decision; He thought about what he needed to do to achieve his goal. He said to himself, "Well, first of all, I have to make money and I have to find a job to make money ... but with this appearance no one hires me; They think that I am a thief. First, I have to think about my appearance." John wanted to learn French so that he could read the text of the letter himself. He decided to work first and earn money so that he could go to a French class with that money.

That day, he searched so that he might find a job, but he was rejected as soon as they saw his appearance, but John did not give up with the will he had. It was getting dark; John decided to return to his safe place; so, he took the way to the dead-end alley. He felt the same again! But this time he was not afraid at all, and on the contrary, he felt good; Sense of security; it was as if the dumpster was his home.

On the way to the dead-end alley, he thought about how good it would be if he could find the right clothes that he could use to sort himself out so that he might be able to find a good job. It was with these thoughts that he reached the alley and entered the dumpster in the same way. This time John did not wish for any special food, but he hoped in his heart that this time too God would help him and find good food. He smelled again ... he smelled good. After a bit of searching, he found food and he was happy; again, a piece of chicken in the dish with the same gravy on the chicken had fallen into the dumpster. He ate the chicken happily and thanked God for paying attention to him.

John fell asleep thinking, and woke up in the morning, as usual, to the sound of cars. As he rubbed his eyes, his eyes suddenly fell on a piece of clothing that had fallen into the dumpster. He was about to scream in astonishment; john believed that this dumpster was the bucket of wishes. John changed his clothes there, and he happily came out of the wish bucket and was happy that he could ask for money from the wish bucket tonight there was no need to work and walked the streets again, but This time he was walking the streets not to find work and food, but to explore the city ... and he felt that this time he was walking in the streets like a gentleman.

Although he did not eat anything from morning to night, it seemed that the amount of energy that the food in the trash had given him, he could spend until night very easily and not feel hungry...

It was getting dark, and John, who had come out of the dumpster in the morning, was just thinking of a bag full of money that he would find in the bucket tonight and all his problems would be solved. He was happily moving towards the dumpster, and this time, when he reached that alley, that feeling was no longer there and there was no mysterious feeling; He felt that he was no longer familiar with it. He went to the dumpster and climbed out of the box and threw himself into the dumpster, but this time he hit the bottom of the dumpster very quickly and felt severe pain! John said to him, "It must have happened because I opened my eyes!" I have to close my eyes. John was waiting for money and food and started smelling; but there was nothing, and instead of the good smell of food, he could smell the bad smell of garbage.

John did not find any food; He said to himself, "Certainly, because I did not wish what food should be in the dumpster, there is nothing here!" Then he thought, "Well, I had not wished the night before! Maybe every wish lasts only two nights!" Because his thought was more involved with money, he looked for money and said to himself, I can buy better food tomorrow and eat full with the money I find, but the more he searched, the more disappointed he became ...

He got tired after an hour of searching. He thought, "I certainly did not wish correctly that I did not find the money there" and decided to sleep there. That night, the smell of garbage bothered him a lot, but he had to sleep with that smell.

He woke up in the morning and went to the streets very hungry. He had to find something to feed. With a lot of trouble, he could find a piece of dry bread to at least get rid of that state of hunger. He thought about the money again, and this time he wished with more energy maybe the money was in the trash. Night came and John returned to that alley; without fear, he went to the dumpster and threw himself into it, and the dumpster smelled worse than the night before! Although he had closed his eyes, he felt more pain from hitting the bottom of the trash and soon reached the bottom of it. He felt that his hand was injured, but he got up and looked for money, regardless of the wound on his hand; Even food was no longer important to him; He was just looking for money, but it was in vain ... He stopped trying and the bad smell of the dumpster was no longer tolerable; He came out of the dumpster and sat and thought in a corner of the dead-end alley. That the dumpster had lost its magical power? Or there was no magic power at all and it was all an illusion or it was just a normal event!

It was in these thoughts that an idea suddenly came to his mind; He thought about what had happened; He concluded that the magic power of the dumpster had disappeared since the thought of making money effortlessly came to his mind. John found a place to sleep and was able to sleep for a few hours with all the cold and hunger. The next morning, John woke up and decided to go back and find a job. He went to the park, washed his hands and face, brushed his hair, and moved. After going to a few places, he arrived at a French restaurant.

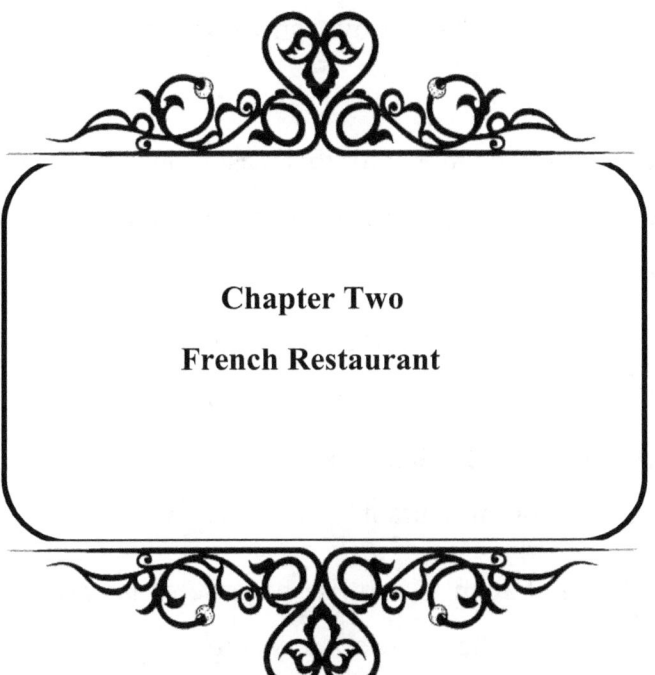

Chapter Two

French Restaurant

The owner of the restaurant was a man with a sullen face, but his eyes showed that he had a kind heart. John came in and said hello. A French man whose name was Jean answered. John's appearance was not the same as before, and they no longer looked at him as a thief or an offender or as a homeless person; for this reason, Jean spoke to John very politely and said, "Yes, boy, can I do something?" "Can I help you"?

It was not time to eat; for this reason, Jean was surprised to see a child the age of John in the restaurant, especially since John was alone.

John began to speak. Very serious and dignified; He looked into Mr. Jean's eyes like a forty-year-old man and said, "Excuse me, sir!"I wanted to know if there was anything I could do in your restaurant".

Jean stared at John in surprise because of his request and said, "You came here to work, my son"!

"Yes," John said.

Jean replied, "But you are too young to work here; By the way, I do not have a job for you; "I have a workforce in all sectors".

John looked at Jean pleadingly and said with sadness in his eyes, "I will do whatever you say. Do not consider my body; I can do anything; Even the hardest and heaviest tasks. Help me for God's sake; "I want to stand on my own two feet".

Jean thought for a moment and said, "Oh, there's nothing I want to do to employ a worker, and at the same time it's not so crowded here that I want to add someone, and you are not old enough to work yet".

John said with great sadness and hatred that had blocked his throat: "Oh ... oh, I can no longer ... I can no longer bear the hunger. Please; I can work as a strong man. I can do whatever your restaurant workers do; please. I do not want much; just some food; I can live on the lowest salary. I need it".

But whatever Jean thought, he did not know what to keep it for, and said with a certain sorrow, "I am sorry"!

After hearing this word, it was as if cold water was poured on his head; He looked at Jean for a moment and said, "Thank you".

John had hopes of getting a job at this restaurant. Although he had gone to many other places and had not been accepted, he felt different here and thought he could work here. John started walking down the three entrance steps of the restaurant; he pushed the doorknob down and tried to step out, when suddenly Jean called out, "My son, come back".

John turned happily and quickly back and said, "Can I stay, sir"?

Jean replied, "I do not know which part to put you; I have not thought about it yet, but I want to keep you; It's as if someone is telling me that you are useful to me. You can work here, but you do not get paid much; Not much work here; I give you food, but think of a place to sleep for yourself; you cannot sleep here. You do not have one more meal. You start work at six in the morning; We had lunch at noon; We rest for three hours and come again for dinner until eleven o'clock at night. "After that you are free, go wherever you want".

John was overjoyed and said to Jean with the same joy and excitement, "Make sure you do not regret it. I can be a good employee for you; I promise you this. "I will be here tomorrow at six o'clock in the morning."

"Very well," said Jean. You can go, but I still do not know why I did it! God save me from my sympathies! Go my son; I will be waiting for you tomorrow. "I should think and consider a place for you until tomorrow".

John happily left the restaurant and walked around the restaurant to remember the surrounding streets. Although he was hungry, great happiness made him forget hunger. It was slowly getting darker. John thought that because he no longer thought of making money effortlessly; so, the dumpster is working properly. He hurried to a special alley, this time dreaming of a piece of juicy steak. He rushed to the dumpster. When he reached it, he stood for a few minutes and asked God if the power of the dumpster was correct. He stepped on the box with a few steps and climbed up and slowly threw himself into the dumpster. It slowly reached the bottom of the bucket as it fell into the valley for a long time; John noticed that the power of the dumpster had returned, and as soon as he reached the bottom, he began to sniff and smell the steak, and began to search. After finding the steak, he began to eat with indescribable enthusiasm. John had never felt better than this before, and he felt he was the happiest person on earth, and he thanked God.

That night, John fell asleep thinking about the restaurant and woke up early in the morning; He went to the park near the alley, washed his hands and face, and moved to the restaurant. On the way, he thought about how the staff would treat him and how he was accepted as a young man! He was in these thoughts that found him in front of a restaurant; It was still fifteen minutes to six o'clock. With enthusiasm, John took his steps very quickly and arrived at the restaurant a little earlier. He had to wait until six o'clock to enter the restaurant.

There was a bridge in front of the restaurant, under which the river flowed into the city; John climbed the bridge and watched the sunshine and the play of light in the river. It was six o'clock in the morning. John moved to the entrance of the restaurant and knocked on the door. He stood for a moment; when he heard no sound, he knocked again. After a moment's delay, the sound of someone walking on the wooden floor of the restaurant was finally heard, who said in a sleepy voice, "Who is there?" Wait a moment; I am coming. What do you want this morning? Blimey...! They don't stop early in the morning. "I am coming ... I am coming."

The sound of the man's slow footsteps indicated his old age. John was a little stressed; He did not know what the man was like and how he should treat the man.

The door finally opened, and John met a man about seventy years old on the doorstep. The man's face was full of wrinkles and his hands were callused, which was a sign of hard work. John was appraising the man; From the tip of the foot to the top of the head. At one point he met the look of a man who was looking at him angrily.

John got himself together and said, "Excuse me, I ... I'm John Wilson. Yesterday I talked to the gentleman in charge here; I was supposed to work here from today. He told me to work from six o'clock in the morning; "That's why I disturbed you at this time".

The old man, named Jack Havins, looked at John a little surprised and a little angry, and said, "Mr. Truffaut said about you yesterday that you were going to come here. So, you are that boy! Come and sit on that chair by the window. Mr. Truffaut comes in at seven o'clock and explains what you have to do. Until then, sit here and do not move and do not touch anything. "Did you understand"?

"Yes, sir......," John said.

"I'm Havins," Jack said. "Jack Havins." And he walked slowly from the door so that John could enter.

Jack entered the restaurant and stood a little further ahead, and Mr. Havins closed the door, pointed to the chair, and motioned for John to sit on it. John moved to the chair and sat down on the chair.

"Be careful ... I'm paying attention here," Mr. Havins said as he walked slowly toward the door that he came out. If you move or want to touch something, I will come here immediately; "Did you understand"?

"Yes, Mr. Havins," John said in a trembling voice.

The chair he was sitting in was by the window, from which the golden branch of the sunlight, shining into the hall, illuminating a piece of ground; Some of the light had fallen on his face and lit up his face. John's innocent face looked much more beautiful in the sunlight. Despite the fatigue and hardships of life, John still had hope in life and knew that God was helping him.

He appraised the hall; Mr. Truffaut's office was there. There were several landscape paintings on the wall. And the painting of the man that showed it belonged to the past. John did not know that the man was Napoleon Bonaparte. Mr. Jean Truffaut had a strong interest in Bonaparte, and considered him as one of the honors of France, and always named Bonaparte with pride. The other painting on the wall was a picture of Mr. Truffaut's youth. On Mr. Truffaut's desk was a picture of himself, his wife, and an eight- or nine-year-old boy in a frame. The boy in the picture did not look very happy. Behind them was the Eiffel Tower, the symbol of

Paris. Other items in the room were desks, telephones, and office supplies. It did not look like a big room and its accessories were cheap.

After examining that room, John turned his attention to the outside; People were slowly starting to move. From there, the view of the river was more beautiful. John looked at the people who were crossing the bridge, coming and going and greeting each other. It was as if they were from the same neighborhood and knew each other.

John came to his senses with the sound of the clock striking seven in the morning. He looked at his watch and realized that it was time for Mr. Truffaut to arrive. He arranged himself, ran his hand through his hair, and waited for Mr. Truffaut to arrive. At that moment, a voice was heard; It was Mr. Truffaut who turned the key in the lock. The door opened and Mr. Truffaut entered. At that moment, Mr. Havins entered from another room and said, "Good morning, Mr. Truffaut. Welcome. "The boy you talked about yesterday is waiting for you in the room."

It was as if Mr. Havins was no longer the same seventy-year-old man! It was a little faster.

"Oh," said Mr. Truffaut. I forgot; I told the boy to be here at six in the morning. I have lost my consciousness as I'm so busy".

He took a few steps to the room and entered. Seeing Mr. Truffaut, John got up and said, "Hello, Mr. Truffaut. Good morning. "I have been sitting here since six in the morning, waiting for you to tell me what to do".

"Yes, yes, my son, I know," said Mr. Truffaut. I forgot this morning that I told you to be here at six o'clock. Okay! No matter. You are helping to clean the restaurant from today. You sweep here. You wash the dishes and move the tables; In short, you work with Richard and you do whatever he tells you. Be careful, if you break or sabotage something here, I will reduce your salary. "Go with Mr. Havins now to introduce Richard to you and show you the location of your job".

Then he shouted at Mr. Havins, "Havins, Havins!" Come here, take this boy and show him where he works; "Then leave it to Richard to explain his work to him".

A few moments later, Mr. Havins appeared in front of the door. John walked to the door and went with Mr. Havins to see Richard. John wished Richard was a good person to work with. John and Mr. Havins headed for the door and went down the stairs. John counted the stairs; It was eight stairs to the kitchen, where there were many large cauldrons with stoves still off and people ready to cook. The walls of the kitchen were covered with white tiles that looked clean. John was moving with Mr. Havins. Mr. Havins stood at one point and shouted, "Guys, pay attention for a moment"!

After a moment, everyone turned their attention to Mr. Havins and John. "This boy's name is John," Mr. Havins said. "From now on, he will work with Richard and help clean up here".

Everyone said, "Hello, John." welcome."

"Hello everyone," John said happily. "I am happy to work here".

"All right, everyone, go to your work," Mr. Havins said. Then he called to Richard, "Richard, come here; "I need to talk with you."

A sixteen- or seventeen-year-old boy came with a smile on his face. " This is John, and from now on you will work together." Mr. Havins said. Go and thank God that you have some help from now. Be kind to this boy; "You know that I see you and I am always everywhere".

Richard held out his hand to John and said "Hello, I am Richard and I am happy to work with you from now on".

John shook Richard's hand and said, "Hello."I am also very happy".

"Let me show you the location of your job," Richard said. "We have nothing to do until noon, as customers come".

John and Richard set out to see different parts of the restaurant. First, they went to the dining hall; it was a beautiful hall With the French-style architecture, the paintings on the wall, and the chairs made of high-quality wood, the atmosphere of the dining hall was pleasant. Richard showed the restaurant elsewhere and then they went to the kitchen together. Mr. Gerard was there when they got to the kitchen.

Gerrard, a 45-46-year-old man, was a restaurant chef, who was French. Gerard saw John and asked Richard, "Who is this boy"?

Richard replied, "His name is John and he's going to help me with the cleaning here".

Gerard was a kind-hearted man. He looked at John lovingly. John liked Gerard's loving look. "Hello," Gerard held out his hand. I am Gerard; The chef of this restaurant. "I hope you can have a good time in this restaurant, my son!"

John shook hands and thanked him, and then went with Richard to clean the dining room. It was almost noon, and in a few hours, the customers would come for lunch.

"These are good, good-hearted people," Richard said. After Mr. Truffaut, Mr. Havins is versatile. Mr. Havins has been here with Mr. Truffaut since the beginning of the construction and helped him, and before that, he was with him in France. He looks rough, but he has a kind heart; "In general, it will not be difficult here".

John was happy to be able to work with these people at this restaurant. John and Richard cleaned the dining room tables and floor. The food was prepared in the kitchen and the customers were slowly coming in and ordering food. If the inside of the kitchen got dirty, Richard and John would clean or wash the dirty dishes. After lunchtime was over for the customers, they could eat too. They ate a hearty meal that day. After the meal was over, they started cleaning the hall and preparing it for dinner, and then went to the kitchen. This was repeated every day.

It was eleven o'clock and John no longer had anything to do in the restaurant and said goodbye to everyone to go to his place of sleep. He moved towards the magic dumpster. He was no longer hungry that day because he had eaten a hearty meal. He thought to himself that it was better to wish for a drink; For example, a juice. He reached for the dumpster and climbed up and saw that inside the dumpster was what he wanted. That night he saw Mr. Gerard dream, smiling at him with a kind face and caressing him.

John went to a restaurant the next day and went about his daily business with Richard. As he worked, he thought about how good it would be to learn French from Mr. Gerard. He was overwhelmed by these thoughts when he saw Mr. Gerard with a smile on his face. John replied with a smile and said to Mr. Gerard, "I had a dream last night.

"What sleep?" Said Mr. Gerard. "Was it good or bad"?

" It was good," John said. You all smiled at me; "You caressed me like the truth".

"Good," said Gerard. "When a person loves someone, sleep becomes like reality." Then he put his hand on John's head and said, "I already had a son who was very similar to you; Clever and shrewd, but"...

At that moment, Mr. Gerard's face turned sad, and laughter disappeared from his face, and he said with a little hatred and sigh, "... but he was killed in an accident".

John was very upset to hear this and almost cried. "I'm very sorry to hear that," he said.

"It's been a few years ago," Gerard said. "If he were alive now, he would be the same age as Richard." He put his hand on John's head again and said, "Take care of yourself, my son! If you have a problem, say; "If I can, I will help".

John thanked Mr. Gerard and got to work, and Mr. Gerard returned to the kitchen. After Mr. Gerard left, Richard told John, "Mr. Gerard is a man of kindness and has a pure heart; "I think he likes you".

John thought to himself that he could ask Mr. Gerard to teach French to him French language. If he says why you want to learn, I say I would like to travel to France in the future.

John returned to his usual place and slept calmly that night. In his dreams, he had many dreams and aspirations. He went to the restaurant the next morning, and after cleaning the kitchen, he went to Mr. Gerard and said, "Excuse me, can I ask you something"?

"Yes, son," said Mr. Gerard, "tell me what you want me to do for you."

"Forgive my rudeness," John said. I wanted ... I wanted you to teach me French if possible; "I would love to learn French so that I can go to France in the future and see it".

When Mr. Gerrard saw that John was interested in France and would like to see that country, he said with great enthusiasm: "Of course my son! We do this whenever you want. "When do you want to start"?

"If so, from today," John said.

"Oh," said Mr. Gerard. Okay, very well. "Between working hours when there is no cooking and no cleaning, we can take an hour to learn, and of course, we will start tomorrow".

That night, John went to his home with great joy. He wanted to arrive very early tomorrow so he could start his training. John was happy that things were going as he wanted and he thanked God for that.

The next morning, he woke up early and hurried to the restaurant, and did his work very quickly. Richard was amazed at John's energy! John finished his work and went to Mr. Gerard. But Mr. Gerard said, "Wait for my work to be done." and told John to wait in the hall.

After a while, Mr. Gerard came; He also brought books, notebooks, and pens. He brought them to John and said, "Because I knew it would be difficult for you to prepare these things, I prepared them myself."

John thanked him and then they started the lesson. John listened to the lesson with indescribable enthusiasm and great intelligence, and he understood everything Mr. Gerard said the first time, and there was no need to repeat it. Mr. Gerard congratulated John on his intelligence and perseverance. An hour of the class ended very quickly, and Mr. Gerard said it would be better to go and eat something so that we could work for the rest of the day, and he gave John the book and said, "Whenever you learn some words, you can practice at night from this book".

John picked up the book and thanked Mr. Gerard again. John that night, before going to bed sleeping, thought about the lesson he had learned that day and repeated the words to himself until he fell asleep. When he woke up in the morning, he said to himself, I wish I could go to the bathroom. When he went to the restaurant, Mr. Truffaut said, "You can use the bathroom here whenever you want, and John was very happy to get to whatever he was thinking or wishing for".

Days passed and John worked French with Mr. Gerard every day and he got better every day. John progressed much faster than the others with his intelligence. After a few months, Mr. Gerard spoke to John little by little in French so that John could speak better. During this time John had collected the money he had received from Mr. Truffaut.

One day Mr. Truffaut asked John where he lived, and John gave the address of the alley, but Mr. Truffaut did not know that there were no houses in that alley at all; In fact, John himself did not know why there is such an alley that is not even surrounded by a house.

Six months later, John was still not ready to read the letter; Both according to the French language and financially. If there is something in the letter that requires travel, he should be able to pay its cost. He had decided not to open the letter until he had earned enough money, but since he had been able to learn some French, he was tempted to read the letter some nights, but he controlled himself again.

One day Mr. Gerard asked John what day he was born.

"August 18," John replied.

There were 20 days left until John's birthday and the weather was warmer. In the summer, John wished he had a new cloth, and the dumpster generously gave John a new cloth. Since John had lived with a poor family, he had never received a big gift on his birthday, but they still congratulated him, and even if it were possible, they would buy a small gift for John, but from the day he lost his family, there was no one left to congratulate him and John was always alone on his birthday and thinking about the days when he was celebrating his birthday with his family.

A few days before his birthday, John realized that the behavior of the restaurant staff was a little suspicious and that they treated John differently. Richard was constantly keeping john working, trying to keep him busy and only letting John go when it was time for lunch and practicing French until John's birthday.

John congratulated himself when he woke up on the morning of his birthday. After getting up, he went to the park and washed his hands and face, and that day he put on the latest clothes he had dreamed of from the dumpster and went to the restaurant. When he arrived at the restaurant, he was surprised to see that the door of the restaurant was open; he entered the restaurant without knocking and went to the kitchen. When he got to the kitchen, everyone was working. John greeted everyone loudly and everyone answered, but they were working hard. John wondered what they were preparing for that hour of the day! Richard called John again and took him to the dining hall and they got to work. "We never started this time of the morning," John said. What has happened?"

"We have special guests today," Richard said. John shrugged and began to work in surprise.

An hour later Mr. Truffaut came; John and Richard greeted him, and Mr. Truffaut called Richard and talked to him, and then Richard went to the kitchen and told John to continue working there. After a while, Mr. Havins came and talked to Mr. Truffaut, and Mr. Truffaut turned to John and said, "John, come with me." "I need help".

They went to the kitchen; when they reached the bottom of the stairs, they all sang the song "Happy Birthday" and then clapped and spread colored papers in the air.

John was surprised to see this scene and burst into tears of joy, but did not know how to thank his friends. When everyone was quiet, John said, "I did not expect anyone to remember me until they even wanted to congratulate me on my birthday!" "I thank all of you for thinking of me".

"Wait," Richard said. This is just the beginning. Come with me." And then he took John by the hand and they went to the table where the gifts were placed. There was a cake on the table, which was on the cake, candles, according to the age of John. Richard sat John on the chair behind the table and lit the candles.

He asked John to make a wish and blow out the candles. John had a great dream in his heart; He wished he could discover that black object and wished he knew the person in the photo and found the place behind the photo. Then he blew the candles with power and turned all the candles off. His friends clapped for him and gave him the gifts they had prepared.

Richard had whistled a gift. Mr. Gerard gave a book of French fiction, some money, and a compass, Mr. Havins a good pen and a notebook, but most importantly Mr. Truffaut...

"My gift is here," Mr. Truffaut said. "You have to come with me to see the gift I want to give you."

John got up and walked with Mr. Truffaut; the others walked and reached the end of the kitchen. At the end of the kitchen was a door that led to the kitchen staff room where they slept at night. They all came in, and Mr. Truffaut pointed to a room and said, "This is your room from tonight; They all helped to prepare it right here. The reason why they did not allow you to come to the kitchen for a long time was that they would prepare it for you during the rest hours. They tried as hard as they could to make room for you. I heard that you do not have a good place to sleep; that's why I decided to make a place for you right here. Well, this is also my gift; "I hope you like it".

John could not speak because he was so happy, and at that moment he looked into Mr. Truffaut's eyes, and at one moment he hugged Mr. Truffaut tightly and thanked Mr. Truffaut with tears in his eyes.

Mr. Truffaut touched John's head and said, "Wipe away the tears; "From now on, the hardships are over".

John parted ways from Mr. Truffaut and thanked all his friends who had helped prepare the place; Then they all went to the kitchen to eat cake and then got to work. John and Richard were also cleaning the kitchen, which had become dirty for John's birthday party.

After a long time, John would sleep under a roof that night and could sleep in a bed without the cold and worry. John was thinking of the magic dumpster when he went to bed. He decided to see it for the last time tomorrow night and go into the dumpster. John thought he wished something worthwhile to dumpster prepare for him and then went to sleep...

In the morning, he woke up to the sound of Richard calling to him to get ready for work. John got up, put on his work clothes, and went to work. The others were getting ready for work. John worked with energy and joy. That night, Mr. Truffaut allowed him to leave a little earlier to collect his belongings from his previous residence. Mr. Truffaut said he could leave if Richard had no problem. John got permission from Richard and did his job earlier, and at nine o'clock he headed for the alley. On the way, he was still thinking about his dream. First, he wanted to wish for the last food he wanted to eat there. John had eaten a small meal that day so that he could eat the food the dumpster gave him at night; John wished for different foods and then thought about his main dream and came to the conclusion that he could find a clue to that photo. He reached the alley and entered the dumpster; there he came across a variety of foods and drinks and a gift! It was as if the dumpster had prepared a gift for John on his birthday. John opened the gift quickly; there were binoculars, a small camera, and a book.

John was happy with the gift he received and thanked God. After opening his gift, he thought of his dream and began to search for clues, but whatever he looked for, he found nothing. He thought to himself, maybe he should find his way. The square's alarm clock rang eleven times and John realized it was time to leave; Because if it was late, the restaurant staff would go to bed, and he would have to sleep out that night, and John did not want this to happen at all; So he got up and came out of the dumpster, then looked at the dumpster and said goodbye. He thanked the dumpster from the bottom of his heart and left.

John had reached the end of the alley. He turned to see that alley for the last time, but the alley was slowly disappearing. John ran to the alley, but hit a wall hard and fell. He got up and put his hand on his head and looked at the alley; the alley was gone! And there was only a wall! And he could not find anything by touching the wall. John realized that alley was magical too! After a few moments, he remembered that he had to go to the restaurant and move on. He arrived at the restaurant after thirty minutes. Richard was waiting for him to open the door. John thanked him when he saw that Richard was awake because of him.

John had not talked to anyone about the dumpster story, and he could not tell Richard what had happened and where he was, so he could share some of his consternation with someone. He went to his bed and fell asleep with all the questions in his mind.

He woke up the next morning and went to work. During the break and after the French class, he remembered last night's gifts and quickly went to his gifts. First, he took a few pictures with his camera and then he looked at different places with his binoculars, but because that space was closed, he could see nothing but the wall and then he picked up the book; The book was in French. John began reading that book because he had almost learned to read. It was a cookbook, but it was too old. In that book, John saw an old French food recipe that, despite working in a French restaurant, he had never heard of or eaten. John was surprised to receive such a gift and put his gifts in the closet and went to the hall to do things.

It was night and John went to bed. As he lay down, he wondered why the dumpster didn't give him a clue to that photo. Why did his wish not come true? And what did these gifts mean? Why was that book given to him as a gift? He suddenly thought that he could use this book to make original French food. Maybe in this way, he can help Mr. Truffaut's restaurant, which the number of its customers was decreasing day by day. John had seen Mr. Truffaut talking to Mr. Havins and Gerard about the problem. Mr. Gerard cooked good food, but it was not very special, and could not distinguish Mr. Truffaut's restaurant from other restaurants. They thought that if this happened, they would have to close the restaurant, and they did not know what the staff would do if the restaurant closed.

John was always worried about going back to the past. When he thought about it, he happily got up, took the book out of the closet again, and began to read under the dim light that shone from the street lamp into the corner of the bed. Inside the book were more than a hundred recipes. After some study, John thought about how to discuss this with Mr. Gerard so that he would not doubt the book. After some thought, he concluded that he could say that he had a grandmother who knew these foods and always wanted John to write down the recipe for these foods, and because he was writing down the recipe for these foods, they have reminded in his mind. As for being French, he can say that his grandmother's mother was French and John is of French origin.

John slept that night, and the next morning, after finishing his work, at the time of the French class, and after the end of the class, he raised the matter with Mr. Gerard, and said that

I knew the recipe for a series of French foods which I had learned from my grandmother and gave the necessary explanations.

"So why do we have to make such food?" Mr. Gerard said after hearing John speak.

"It makes the restaurant have different foods than others and people come here to try new foods," John said.

Mr. Gerard thought well of John; He wanted to try what John said, but because he was a chef and his pride did not allow him to tell others that he did not know this French recipe, he did not want to allow John to do it. That is why he did not accept and said, "No, I do not think this is right; because we may lose some of our customers."The taste of these foods may not be in line with the tastes of new people because they are old and they will not accept it".

Although he had never eaten such food before, John said, giving Mr. Gerard a reason: "I used to eat it when my grandmother used to make it; it's so delicious."I'm sure it's right".

"Anyway, I have to think a little bit to see if I can do it," said Gerard, who did not know what decision to make. "It's better to go back to work," he continued. And he went to the door.

John felt that Mr. Gerard was a little upset, but he sincerely wished he would accept. John felt that this could help the restaurant. He thought that the book had not reached him for no reason; "So he must use it".

It had been three days since Mr. Gerard had spoken to John. Mr. Gerrard, as before, did not speak warmly, and the French class was no longer on time. During those three days, Mr. Gerard no longer paid much attention to cooking, and the food sometimes became salty, and sometimes without salt and the customers became fewer than before, and Mr. Truffaut was more worried than before.

Mr. Gerard finally made up his mind on the fourth day and spoke to John in French class; "We were doing this," he said. Of course, I still think this is not right, but I do not know why I listen to a boy; Anyway, I don't think it will make the restaurant any worse, but you should not tell anyone that you are giving me this recipe. "I am asking Mr. Truffaut to take you to the kitchen as an assistant chef, and from now on, you work with me".

" Ok Mr. Gerard's," John said happily. Thank you for trusting me; "Be sure that I will answer your trust and everything will be fine".

Confused, Mr. Gerard got up and went to the door and said, "I will go to Mr. Truffaut's office and tell him this; "I hope he will accept".

Mr. Gerard went to Mr. Truffaut's office and discussed the matter with him. He was surprised by this request but accepted it for Mr. Gerard. From that day on, John had to work in the kitchen with Mr. Gerard. Richard was a little upset, too, but John relieved his sadness by talking to him, and John promised to help him when he was free...

Chapter Three

Cook Book

That day came and John was a little stressed about how to do the recipes so he could make good food. Everyone looked at John in amazement; In particular, the cook's mates who looked bad. John was walking with Mr. Gerard. "Today, John is helping me with cooking," said Mr. Gerard; I want to turn John into an expert chef to replace me in the future. No one should bother him; did you understand?" Everyone answered, yes, Mr. Gerard.

John had given the list of supplies to Mr. Gerard and Mr. Gerard to the purchaser. John, in turn, told Mr. Gerard what to do; John and Mr. Gerard, apart from the others, were on a special pot for cooking. John started with the first recipe he wrote on paper. The food was for the night, and finally, after a few hours of activity and care, the food was prepared.

"Well," Mr. Gerard said, "now I have to try it. First, see if it tastes like your grandmother's food." John did not know what the food should taste like, but confident in the book and what he had done, he took a spoon and tried some of it. With the first spoon he put in his mouth, his eyes flashed ... The taste he had tried he had never seen in any food; it had an extraordinary taste. "I'm sure when customers eat this food, they're not fed up with it anymore, and they still like to come here," John said.

Mr. Gerard became curious and tasted it himself, and as he tasted the food, he shouted for joy, and the others turned and looked at them, and then turned to him and said, "Well done, my son! This food is wonderful. I have not tasted such a taste in all these years of cooking ... great! "There is only one problem."

"What's wrong?" John asked.

Mr. Gerard said: "For some time now, the customers have been decreased and it can be said that it has reached zero; "I do not know how to get them here." "Well, it doesn't matter," John said With ads. "Richard and I go to the door and invite people to try the original French food here."

Mr. Gerard thought for a moment and then said, "We must first consult with Mr. Truffaut and ask him to taste this food."Stay here until I go to Mr. Truffaut's office." And then he moved to the office.

When John was alone, he felt the heavy gaze of the other people in the kitchen. John lowered his head so as not to have to look into the eyes of others or be asked a question that he had to answer. A few minutes later, Mr. Gerard and Mr. Truffaut entered the kitchen and went to the pot together; Mr. Gerard gave Mr. Truffaut a spoonful of food, and after tasting, it said, "This is wonderful ... great! I have tasted this taste once in the past when I was very young; I still remember that taste under my tongue; This is the same taste and of course more delicious; Because a professional chef like you made it. Mr. Gerard, this is great! Why are you late? Do what you said. Hurry up, John. Go and invite people to the restaurant with Richard. Surely, if they taste such a taste once, they will come here again. "John ... you are still here!"

John hurried to change his clothes and followed Richard, explaining to him what Mr. Truffaut had ordered. After Richard changed his clothes, they went outside to work. After an hour, they finally managed to lead a few people into the restaurant to order the same food after the waiter advertised the chef's special food.

Mr. Gerard, Mr. Truffaut, and John watched from a distance to see how the customer reacted after eating! Do they like special food or not? Customers' faces showed that they were satisfied with the food; this can also be seen from the reward paid to the waiter.

"From tomorrow, this food will be added to the menu," Mr. Gerard said.

John decided to try one food every day; "Tomorrow is a new meal," he told Mr. Gerard. Mr. Gerard also shook his head with a smile and expressed his positive opinion.

From that day on, until they followed all the instructions in the book, new meals will be cooked each time, and old foods were removed from the menu altogether and replaced with new ones. Mr. Gerard wrote down all the recipes so that he would not have a problem if John was not there. The restaurant is getting more crowded every day; As Mr. Truffaut was forced to recruit new staff. Mr. Truffaut, on Mr. Gerard's recommendation, had tripled John's salary, although he was not very satisfied with it. The kitchen was very busy and John's work was very hard during the day; so, he didn't have a chance to think about other things. John was slowly becoming a skilled cook. As John told the recipes to Mr. Gerard, he sometimes did it himself and could make some of the food himself. Everyone was both happy and sad that the number of orders had increased; they were happy that the restaurant was no longer closed, and they were upset that their duty had increased, but their salaries had not changed. It has been more than a year since John came to that restaurant. During this time he made many friends and was closest to Richard; because they worked together at the same time and were closer in age; Also with Mr. Gerard; although very different in age, they talked like two friends and sometimes communed with each other. Although young, John behaved like a man in his forties.

One day, John counted his money and realized that he had enough money to travel with. It was time to read the letter; so he decided to take the black object somewhere outside the restaurant and read the letter. That night he took leave from Mr. Truffaut for tomorrow.

"There is no problem," Mr. Truffaut said. You have not taken a day off since the day you came here; "Go and excursion for yourself."

John thanked Mr. Truffaut. That day, Mr. Truffaut was very happy with the high sales of the restaurant, and he leaned back in his chair, put his pipe in the corner of his mouth, and smoked the pipe happily.

After leaving Mr. Truffaut's office, John went to Mr. Gerard to tell him that he was on leave tomorrow so that he could be informed. After seeing Mr. Gerard, John told him about it, and Mr. Gerard gave him a hundred-dollar bill. John thanked Mr. Gerard and went to his room.

The next morning he left the restaurant to read the letter and also take a walk around the city. John decided to go sightseeing first and then read the letter. He wanted to spend some of the money he had received from Mr. Gerard for fun; So he decided to go to the amusement park and take his time there until noon; So he went to the amusement park and had lunch there, and it was noon when he went to a solitude park so that he could read the letter. He sat on the bench; there was almost no one in the park except for a few people sitting on a bench a long-distance away reading a newspaper.

John was very excited to read the letter; That he did not know what was waiting for him and waited for it for a year and learned French because of it ... He took a few deep breaths and tried to take the stress away from himself. And he took the black object out of his pocket. The black object shone in the sunlight and the reflection of the light hit John's eye. When John saw his name on the black object again, he thought ... He had already examined the object thoroughly and had found nothing but the letter and the photo behind it. He opened the back of it and took the letter and the photo and looked at it again and realized more and more that he was similar to that photo.

John used its back to see his face so that he could compare himself to the man and woman in the photo. He looked at the photo a little and looked at himself a little, but did not find anything; He sighed and put his hand on his face in the photo. Suddenly something happened and the object moved a little and came forward! John looked at it in surprise...! The metal object was slightly away from its metal plate, but with the rods attached to the base, there was a protective metal plate behind the object where John saw himself in it, but there seemed to be another gap between the black object and the metal plate. John looked carefully; the paper seemed to be there, but John's finger did not go into the gap; John's fingers had thickened as he worked, and he could not remove the paper. He found a piece of wood and finally, after a little effort, was able to pull the paper out of the gap. After pulling out the paper, he looked inside again to see if there was anything else? He bent the object so that if there was anything, it would fall out ... As he bent the object; the sound of something hitting the ground was heard. John followed the sound ... a gold coin that looked very old! John shook the black object again, but there was nothing else inside. John examined the object once more and touched it everywhere so that it might not be another hiding place, but it was nothing else. He thought of the paper he had found and opened it; the letter was addressed to him! The script of that letter was similar to that of his mother ... he began to read.

Chapter Four

Mothers Letter

Hello my dear son, John

By the time you read this letter, I am probably no longer in this world; Because I do not dare to tell you the contents of this letter while I am alive. My dear John, inside the container in your hand, there is a letter and a photo hidden behind the container. You have probably seen it and it comes with a letter from an Old Testament gold coin that belongs to you; Of course, I only had one coin and I do not know if there are more coins or not, and if so, I do not know exactly where it is so I can tell you to find it. The man and woman you see in this photo are your real parents, and the real name of the man you see in the photo is "François Wilson," and that woman is your mother. You must have noticed your similarities with them.

Your mother was a very honorable person and she loved you very much. When you were a kid, we lived next door in an old neighborhood. One day, your father found the paper behind the object in the same way, from his father's old furniture, and read it. That letter describes your past and your past generations and shows what your origins were, how much you owed, or where it's now. Your father was persuaded to find the treasure by reading this letter; Your mother first opposed your father, but your father thought only of that treasure and nothing else, saying that this treasure was our right and should be found. Eventually, your mother agreed and let him go, but only for a month and if he could not find it, he must return. Your father accepted and provided the means of travel to find that treasure, and left the next day. Your father followed the treasure, but there was no news about your father for two months. During this time, your mother would sometimes come to us, and sometimes I would go to her so that she would not be alone until finally, the phone rang; it was your father. Emily, your mother, picked up the phone and heard your father's voice and she was happy that your father was alive, but your father said just one sentence, "I'm coming," and hung up. Your very worried mother thought that something had happened to your father who had spoken like that ... Three days passed from that phone call until one night your father entered the room at two o'clock in the morning, without knocking....

That night, François announced that some people were looking for him. Your father had gone to different places to find that treasure so that he could find a clue, but nothing was found and he had to seek help from someone; your father explained that I told the subject of the letter to a fellow traveler I had known for a long time, and that was my biggest mistake. After I found part of that treasure, I had to give another part to that man; That is, Daniel Dallahan, but it was not the whole treasure...

Your father found out from that letter that he had found a small part of that treasure and most of it was on an island that he did not know where. He also found there the black object you see now. The total number of coins was one hundred, which he gave to the Dallahan and took the rest himself, But this was just the beginning; Because Dallahan was more greedy than that and wanted to take the rest of the coins from François; Dallahan also realized that these were not all coins and that there must be something else, he thought François had taken them. Dallahan did not know that this treasure existed elsewhere; For this reason, he plotted to steal those coins and other things that François had.

Your father thought this was likely to happen and he was careful not to be surprised. After returning from the first trip, your father goes to someone who can sell those coins and turn them into money. He puts that money in the bank and opens an account in your name and comes home. All this time, Dallahan has been chasing François to carry out his plan at an opportune time. Your father rests that night, and the next day tells Emily that we must pack up and go to another city so that the matter is forgotten and the Dallahran can get rid of the coins. Your father kept this coin and hid it where you can see it. He believed that this object had a special power, but he did not know how to use its power. The name you see engraved on the black object is the name of your paternal grandfather. But that night, Dallahan executes his plan and attacks the house with two others; when your father notices that they are coming, he asks Emily to come to our house so that he can join them after collecting the necessary items. François gives the object to Emily and asks her mother to take great care of it. Emily insists they go together, but François does not notice. And Emily runs out the back door and makes her way to our house.

At midnight, our doorbell rang; as the door opened, Emily hurried inside. He hugged you tightly and shivered; Without asking what happened, I put your mother on a chair and brought her a glass of water to calm her down a little; she was shaking and excited and out of breath. She said nothing and stared at the ground. Fifteen minutes later, the sound of gunfire came; once ... twice ... three times, and finally with the fourth shot, there was silence. I saw two people running out of the window, and then they got in the car and left quickly ... They passed from in front of our house while running away; I think they saw me in front of the window too. I came to myself with the sound of your crying and saw

Emily lying on the ground unconscious. I picked her up and we lay on the bed with my husband. She was unconscious for several hours. Fifteen minutes after the shooting, police were there and people had gathered. My husband and I went out to see what happened! The police took out the body of a man and that man was your father, but there was no other person ... After the ambulance left, the police dispersed the people and we returned home. When we returned, we saw Emily waking up and sitting on the bed, holding her head in her hands and crying. I realized that your mother understood everything. I wanted to ask Emily about it, but she was not feeling well at all...

The next day, a police investigation began. Because we were your neighbors, they came to us first ... At your mother's request, we left the room and the police spoke only to your mother, and then they asked us questions and left. Your mother said there was one, but there were two who also had guns and were shot in the heart of François.

A month after that incident, your mother, who could not go to that house, asked me to sell it. After selling the house, she called me one morning and said, "Pay close attention to what I have to say, and remember everything I have to say, and if you think you forget it, write it down." » Then she gave me a pen and paper and started talking; Your mother told me about the black object and what your father had done and what had happened that night. And then she handed me the bank book and continued: "This account book, which was opened in the name of John, was opened by François and some money from the coin sale was transferred to this account; "I also transferred the money for the sale of the house to this account yesterday." And she gave me a letter and said: "This is my will; yesterday I went to the lawyer's office and arranged it. I have explained in the letter that after my death, you will take care of John; Of course, I'm sorry that I did not ask your permission before to do this at all, but because I have no one and since it is not clear how long I will live, I did it myself; "I hope you will forgive me for taking this responsibility on you." The next day, Emily was silenced forever as she sat in a chair staring out the window at Building 326.

We buried Emily next to François's grave. Police said Emily's death was a heart attack, but they had not yet concluded François.

I shared all of Emily's advice with Stuart, and we decided to take care of you, and your maintenance expenses would be covered by the same bank account. Stewart and I decided that when you grew up, we would say that Stewart is not your father, and later, if you remember, we told you the same thing, but we did not say anything about your mother; because I wanted you to be a little older.

 In those days a man, possibly Dallahan, came to your house and asked for more inquiries from me. Stuart and I told everything to the police and moved from one house to another house for more security. Dear John, this was the story of your life and that was all I wanted to tell you over the years, but I could not. Your bank account is in New York Mellon's Bank, and when you reach legal age, you can withdraw from that account, and with that credit card, you can meet your needs. The amount is enough for you to have a good life with it, but the booklet and the card are in the safe deposit in the same bank. The key to the safe is in the same pot I always put in front of the entrance. There is a separate part under the pot that has no soil; Break that part and take the key and take the booklet and the card from the safe. And in the end, I apologize for not telling you this during this time; I tried hard, but it didn't work. Know that I loved you as much as your mother, Emily, and so did Stuart; we love you. Dear John, I hope you are successful wherever you are.

Your lovers, Rose and Stewart

John's eyes were filled with tears, and tears dripped down his hands as he read the letter; Hands that showed years older than his age as a result of work. He folded the letter and put it inside the black object, cleaned his face, and looked at the sky. He thought for hours about the contents of that letter, about Rose and Stewart, about Emily and François, and about his own story, how strange and unbelievable it was. He had forgotten the first letter, which was in French; He had completely forgotten why he came here. After a few hours, he noticed the darkness. It was then that he just remembered the subject of the original letter, but he had no desire to read the letter, especially since his father had died because of it.

John remembered the bank they had opened an account for him. He remembered Rose and Stewart being killed in the same bank. He told himself that there must be a connection between their death and the bank robbery, especially since the bank thief had not been caught and the thief had managed to escape. He put both letters and coins in his closet and decided to return to the restaurant due to the darkness approaching eleven o'clock. John decided not to read the letter for a few days to read it at the right time.

It had been a long time since mealtime and John was feeling very exhausted. When he went to the restaurant, he asked Richard to bring him food. Mr. Gerard and Truffaut had left that hour of the night, and no one was in the kitchen; Mr. Havins had gone to sleep, and only Richard was awake, waiting for John to come. John was eating when Richard said with great enthusiasm, "tell; where did you go? How was it? It was fun?" John was impatient, but for Richard not to notice, he showed himself happy and said, "I had a great time today ..." and told the story of going to the amusement park. Richard was so eager to go sightseeing that he asked John to go with him once, and John agreed.

After eating, John thanked Richard and asked to let him wash the dishes, but Richard refused and said you are tired and go rest. John thanked Richard again and went to his room to rest.

John lay on his bed. He was thinking about that letter and what had happened to him and what he should do next. He thought about the credit card and how to get the key! He could not take leave again for tomorrow; Because Mr. Truffaut might be upset and not let him, so he decided to wait a week and then apply for leave, during which he would assess all aspects of the work to get that key. John hoped that the pot would still be in place, and he fell asleep with the same thoughts.

The next morning, he resumed his usual activities and only worked all day long, but as soon as he ended his work again, the same old thoughts and memories came to his mind. The French classes were over, and Mr. Gerard had said that there was no need for further training and that from then on, they would simply speak in French. A week passed like this, and John had no plan in mind; it was better to go to that old house first to see who lived there; then he decides about the pot. At that time, John watered the pot every day; that's why he knew the pot so well.

The days were passed hardly for John. He was just waiting for this week to end and get the key to open the safe with it.

The promised day has finally arrived; John, exhausted, went to Mr. Truffaut that night and asked for leave. Mr. Truffaut frowned a little and said, "Last week you went on leave, boy! Why are you going on leave one after another! What's going on"?

"Mr. Truffaut, I have something to do related to the past, and I have to go and solve that problem," John said. "Otherwise I would not have gone".

Mr. Truffaut glanced at John to see the truth of John's words from his face, but nothing was found. Although he was not satisfied with giving him leave, after a little thought and considering the matter, he said: "Okay, you can go, but be aware that there will be no more leave for another month, and also inform Mr. Gerard that you want to go. If he has no problem, you can go".

John thanked Mr. Truffaut and went to get Mr. Gerard's permission; Mr. Gerard had no problem with John leaving. Richard was there when he wanted to talk to Mr. Gerard, and when he saw that John wanted to go on leave again, he brought himself to John and said, "We were not supposed to go this time together; "So why do you want to go alone?" Richard said this sadly. There was sadness in the tone of his voice and his look. When John saw that Richard was upset about this, he did not know what to say to satisfy him and to make it up to him...

"Dear Richard, I did not take time off for fun," John said. Tomorrow I have a personal job that is related to my past and I must go and do it; you know I just went out for fun. I did not want to take leave again so soon; Mr. Truffaut did not want to take leave either, but because I asked so much, he accepted. Richard, do not be upset with me; "Be sure that

I will not have fun without you, and the next time I will take you with me".

Richard was very kind; On the other hand, he was very clement and forgiving. When John spoke like that, Richard was satisfied and accepted John's words and wished John success and they said goodbye to each other and John went to his room to sleep and wake up early tomorrow morning so that he could do his work; Because he knew that Mr. Truffaut would no longer give him leave and that John had no plans to leave at that time; So he decided to do what he wanted to do tomorrow, anyway.

Early in the morning, before the others woke up, he woke up and left the restaurant. John went to their old house where they used to live. About two hours later he reached the area near the house. In the same old neighborhood, all the memories of the past came alive and passed before his eyes like a movie. It was as if it was only yesterday that John was cycling in the same alleys with his friend Ted. John had not been here since Rose and Stuart died. Seeing those alleys, he thought for a moment and then found himself in front of an old house, all over the building full of memories for John. John loved that house very much; because all of John's childhood memories were there. He looked around the building to see if anyone lived there. The house seemed empty and no one lived in it, but John was afraid to go inside and someone would see him. Went to the hedge in front of the door; He looked at the pot place from a distance and saw a pot with dried flowers in front of the door. It seems that no one has been there for a long time and it is deserted.

John dared a little and decided to go inside the house and pick up the pot; So, he went in and went to the entrance and looked around. No one seemed to be there. He picked up the pot and headed for the entrance to the hedge. As he came out, the front door opened, and a tall, broad-shouldered boy came out with brown hair, light brown eyes, and two rabbit teeth that distinguished him by his large body .

The boy came to John, and when he reached him, he took John by the hand and said, "Where are you going, boy"?

John knew him as soon as he saw him. He was Ted; Childhood friend; When John lived there. John smiled and looked at Ted. "Why are you laughing?" Ted said. "It's like you want to get a real beating"...

Ted has been like that since he was a child. Because of his large body, no one dared to challenge him. Because John was next door to Ted and he was thin, he was friends with Ted, and Ted always was supporting John not to be bothered by someone, and John was always happy to have such a friend.

"You did not know me, Ted Robbins!" Said, John.

"Should I know your little boy !?" Ted said.

"You have not changed yet," John said. "Like in the past, a bully"...

"What do you say, boy?" Ted said. Where did you come from to know me! How do you know my name! Hmmm ... Of course, in this and other neighborhoods, when the name "Ted Robbins" comes up, everyone is shaking. You must know me. But tell me, who are you that you came here and how did you dare to take the pot from the house in front of us? Ha ... boy, I'm been watching you for an hour and I saw that you are going to go there. Now tell me, why did you take this pot? Hey ... I had a friend who liked this pot very much. Well, say; Why"?

John smiled again and said, "I'm glad you still remember that friend"!

"Well ... What do you have to do with this?" Ted said. "Introduce yourself and say what are you doing here"?

"I'm your old friend, John Wilson," John said.

Ted was shocked to hear John's name and stared at John with wide eyes and looked at him carefully; "He wanted to see if he was right".

"But John is dead," Ted said. He died two years ago; "Under the bridge, he died from the cold".

"Who said that?" Said, John. "Did you see me dead"?

"Do not tell you are john so much," Ted said. "Let it be known first that you are, and then… "

"Do not you remember my face?" John said. "Of course, you are right. In these few years, I have suffered so much that I have changed completely."

"If you're right that you're John," Ted said, "let me see. We had a secret place we always went to hide from others; "Tell me, where is there if you are John"?

John thought for a moment and then said, "Well, of course; In that old factory that is closed in the blind alley that no one dares to go there. It was just you and me going there; "Do you remember Ted"?

Ted release John's hand and hugged him tightly and clung to him, saying three times, "John … John … John"!

"Ted, my hand was breaking," John said. Your strength has already increased! Give me a little less pressure ...

Ted release John and looked at him again and said, "Where have you been, boy ... saying you are dead!" I was looking for you a lot. All these years, I've been thinking about what you're doing. I heard the news of your grandmother's death and that you were sent to an orphanage. Many times, I wanted to come and see you, but I did not; I could not see that my friend had such a situation; On the other hand, I could not bring you to me. You know what my dad's temperament is! My father kept me in this house by force; What if you want to come here too! In short ... then I heard that you ran out of the orphanage and wandered in the alleys and had no place to sleep. There I wanted to find you and bring you to me; I said if my father objected, I would bring to you again; I cannot see my friend like this! I missed you so much, buddy"...

John smiled and said, "I missed you too; my situation is not bad now. I work in a French restaurant. "It's not bad ... I just learned to cook and my salary is good".

Ted put his hand on John's head and said, "Your brain worked well since you were a child; you were not like me to study by force. Honestly, I gave up studying and I do not study anymore; I want to go to car repair work like my dad. I do not think I was made to study! "I better do it".

John looked at his watch and saw that it was better to do his job. He stood up and said to Ted, "I have to go now; I am busy now; I will see you later. If you want to see me, you can come to the French restaurant by the river. I finish work at five o'clock in the afternoon; I can see you. I'm going now; Hope to see you soon".

"I'll come to see you," Ted said. "You did not say why you want this pot for"!

"Well, you said it yourself ... You had a friend who was very interested in this pot," said John Laughing. "Well, I came to get this pot too. Maybe I can revive its flowers".

Ted laughed and said, "You're right, John!" I forgot; Okay, go and take care of yourself. If you have an issue or a problem or someone is bothering you, tell me to come; "Okay boy"!

"Thank you, Ted, for sure," John said. "Take care of yourself." And then he shook hands with Ted and left. John was glad to see Ted and his memories were alive. Ted was the only one left from the past. Seeing that he still remembers him, a happy smile settled on his lips.

John was looking for a secluded place to break the bottom of the pot and take out the key, and the best place was the factory; so, he went to the factory to break the pot. When he arrived at the factory, he felt that someone was looking at him. Looked around a little; There was no one. John said to himself that it must have been imaginary because of this environment. He broke the pot and, as Rose had said, the key was there. He picked up the key. John was upset that his favorite flower was drying up. Then he collected the broken parts of the pot and set off to get away from that place and go to the bank. When he came out, he felt that heavy look again but saw nothing. He came out of that place and moved towards the bank. Shortly afterward, he reached the bank and entered. The bank was very crowded; John did not know how to get to the safe without attracting anyone's attention; because, due to his young age, it seemed strange that he wanted to take something out of that safe. "Excuse me, where is the safe deposit?" He asked the bank guard.

"Why do you want my son?" The guard asked.

"My mother is waiting for me," John said. "I want to go to her".

The guard smiled and said, "At the end of the corridor, on the left, you can find your mother there".

John was happy to have passed the first stage, but he did not know what to say in the next stage; because the bank manager will come with him in the first part of the deposit and then he does not know what to say ... John reached the desired place; the person in charge of that section was standing there. John approached and saw better, to tell the truth; so, he went forward and said, "Hello sir. I'm John Wilson; my mother has a safe here that she put something in for me; some time ago, my parents were killed in a bank robbery. "I came to pick up what was in the safe".

The security guard, who looked serious and law-abiding, looked at John and said, "I was in the bank at the time and the thieves had taken me hostage. It was as if they had not just come to rob the bank and were trying so hard to get something from your father; of course, if you are right! In general, your father got into a fight with those two people for a moment; you know, there were two of them, but they hit hard on your father in the face with a rifle butt, and his cheek broke when he was hit by a rifle butt and drowned in blood. Your father fell to the ground and your mother cried and threw herself next to your father. The man, who lost his mask for a moment as a result of the confrontation, had brown hair and a face with stubble and fiery eyes. I was a short distance from your parents and I saw the man, but I lowered my head in my hands in fear. The assailant quickly took off his mask after separating from your father. He shouted at your father, tell me where it is? Tell me, what did you do about it? I know François gave it to you...

Your father kept saying, I do not know what you are talking about. And again, the man said, well you know what I mean ... Where are the coins? You know very well that I killed François because of those coins, and if you do not show the place of the coins, I will kill you too. I know he gave it to you; I do not know why, but I'm sure it's in your hand. Your father also shouts that François did not give us anything...

The man also said, then you should say goodbye to your wife and a bullet was fired at your father and he said to your mother, well, now it is your turn; Do you say or you want to have the same fate as your husband? Your mother said nothing and just cried and put her head on your father's body. The man was bored and could not stand it anymore; On the other hand, the police were everywhere. The second man had taken the money from the bank and said, let's go ... the police are approaching; we must escape sooner. We got a lot of money from here; let's go soon. The first man said, "Oh, this woman has seen my face ... she is revealing me; It is better to get rid of her or take her with us. And the second man refused to take your mother and said, "She is slowing us down; the police can catch us ... Finally, the man decided and, in a moment, he fired his second shot directly at the poor woman's forehead, and your mother died on that moment, falling on her husband's body and never moving again. The man came to me after making sure he was dead and wanted to kill me too, but his friend told him to let go; You want to kill all the people here! This man has not seen us; let's go. The blood was in front of the eyes of that ruthless thief ... Finally, at the insistence of his accomplice, he accepted that he had nothing to do with me and they quickly ran away from the bank. The whole process lasted fifteen minutes; when they left, the police arrived five minutes later, but it was too late. "We gave them the details of the car to pursue, but it was as if they had stolen another car and fled".

The security guard, drowning in his old memories, did not realize at all that he was talking to John; the child of a man and a woman who was killed in a bank. When he was free from the telling of memories, he turned his head to see John, who realized that John had fallen into a chair next to him and was crying, blaming himself. He thought he had killed Rose and Stuart. The bank clerk was upset that he had shared those memories with John, realized his mistake, and apologized to John. The security guard said to John, "I'm sorry, I do not know why I explained this to you ... I'm stupid! Forgive me my son; this story made me very sad and will always remain in my mind. After that, I can no longer sleep well. Oh, they were in front of my eyes; It was very upsetting. "I am sorry for what happened to them, my son."

John clean his face with the tissue the man had given him and said, "Thank you for complimenting me. I always wanted to know what happened to them; I was suffering because I did not know who killed them and why. Mr"...

"I'm Simpson," the man said.

"Yes ... Mr. Simpson, did you tell the police the details of the man who shot my parents?" John continued.

"Oh, yes," said Mr. Simpson, "I was taken to the police station a thousand times and interrogated; I also told the scene that I had seen a thousand times and all the events and words that had been exchanged, but what a use! They had already fled. I do not know how they did it! Because the police of this city have the best intelligence services! "Again, forgive me for telling you this".

At that moment, a lady came out of the safe and said to Mr. Simpson, "Mr. Simpson thank you." And Mr. Simpson got up and said, "Goodbye, Mrs. Loris; Good luck." After Mrs.

Loris left, Mr. Simpson said to John, "She is a very good lady! She comes here every week and I do not know what she puts in the box! Anyway, it does not matter to me. Well, my son, you said you have a box here; do you have a box password? "Of course, you have to have a key that does not work without a password".

John remembered that in addition to the key, in the pot was also a plastic object that he had hurriedly put in his pocket. He took it out of his pocket and opened it; there was a piece of metal inside that some numbers had engraved on it. "I think I have," John said.

"Very well," Mr. Simpson shrugged. "Come with me ... What is your box number"?

"4257," John said.

"Very well," said Mr. Simpson. "We have to go right." John read the box number from the keychain that hung on the key and guessed it was the box number.

They reached the box. "Give me the key, son," said Mr. Simpson. He brought a similar key and then turned it into a lock. "Well," he said to John, "I have to find something on which you can stand up to reach the box." "You must stay here until I return," he continued.

John stood there looking at the many boxes that were there, wondering how Mr. Simpson knew which box belonged to whom.

Mr. Simpson returned with a chair and said, "I think you can reach my son now. "Well ... come on, stay in it to be able to enter your password." John stood on a chair, took the password out of his pocket, and entered it. When he entered the password, he asked God if the password was correct. He entered the password and Mr. Simpson told him to turn the key. John turned the key. "Well ... put that handle down and I'll go out," said Mr. Simpson. If you have an issue, I'm in front of the door. So ... »

Mr. Simpson went out, and John later opened the safe after making sure he was gone. Inside the safe were the same things her mother had said; That is, the bank book and the bank pass card. John picked up the card; the card password was also written on a piece of paper. He put the notebook in the box; He preferred not to use the money for now and decide later. He raised the handle, turned the key, and put the card in his pocket. He got down from the chair and went to the door. Mr. Simpson was standing there. John went to Mr. Simpson and said, "Mr. Simpson, thank you for helping me." Mr. Simpson replied, "Please, my son! Whenever you have a deal with this bank, I am at your service. "I apologize again for remembering the death of your parents".

"No problem, Mr. Simpson," John said. I have become more tolerant. "I can endure these hardships." And then he reached out to shake Mr. Simpson. Mr. Simpson took John's hand and squeezed it softly, "Wherever you are, good luck my son." take care. I hope that everything in that safe box will bring you happiness. Good luck"!

John thanked and left Mr. Simpson. After John went, Mr. Simpson said to himself, I forgot to ask him what he is doing now and with whom he lives, poor boy! His face showed that he had worked very hard.

John came out of the bank and the first thing he did was go to the ATM to see how much cash he had. He inserted the card into the device and took the balance, and he was very happy to see the balance of the card. It was about $ 3,500 on the card. That was enough for John to travel, but John remembered that he had given up on the trip. He took the card from the device. It was about 4 p.m.; John had not eaten yet and was very hungry. He decided to eat a sandwich and ate as soon as he got there. After eating, he decided to take a walk and made his way to the restaurant. On the way, he felt that someone was following him. John was very scared; He increased his speed. He decided to take the rest of the way by subway and entered the first station and boarded the first train that went near the restaurant. It was a bit crowded and he was more comfortable. He arrived at the restaurant an hour later. It was close to dinner and John was very tired. He did not want to work that night; so, he told Mr. Gerard to go to his room, and Mr. Gerard agreed.

All the hours John had been lying on his bed, thinking about the story of Rose and Stuart being killed, he was concluding that before Dallahan came to him too, he must find the person who killed his original parents, as well as Rose and Stewart, and hand him/her over to the police. John was almost certain that he/she would surely come to him, especially since it had been a while since he had been suspected of following him, and he always felt that a shadow was moving near him.

When John woke up in the morning, he went about his business like any other day. Mr. Gerrard had long been suspicious of John's behavior. Although John behaved in a way that no one noticed, he did not succeed in hiding everything. Mr. Gerard knew something was on John's mind, but he did not know what it was. He decided to ask John what had happened to him that had occupied his mind so much.

That morning when they were alone together and Mr. Gerard made sure that none of the staff were there, as he and John were working, without raising his head, he said to John, "Something has happened to you? » John overwhelmed with his thoughts, did not hear Mr. Gerard. Mr. Gerard raised his voice a little, and this time he said louder, "Is there something wrong with you"?

This voice brought John back to himself and said to Mr. Gerard, "do you mean me?" "Yes, my son, I mean you," said Mr. Gerard. " "Is anyone else here except you and me"!

"I'm sorry," John said. I did not notice; "I was thinking".

"Yes, that's my question," said Mr. Gerard. There's a problem"?

"No, Mr. Gerard, why?" Said, John.

"of course ... Something happened," Mr. Gerard said. I have been monitoring your behavior for a long time. Your behavior has completely changed and it is not clear what you are hiding. It must be very important that it has involved your mind so much. "I think it's related to the leave you took"!

John mumbled a little and said, "No, Mr. Gerard, it does not matter; Do not worry".

"I do not believe that," Mr. Gerard said. With the knowledge that I have gained from you during this time, I know that it must be very important that you become like this; anyway, if you do not want to say, ok; I thought maybe I could help. If you do not want to say, it's up to you, but let me tell you that if you want to continue in this way, gradually, your work deteriorates, and if even I say nothing to Mr. Truffaut, Mr. Truffaut realizes this behavior change and deteriorates. Then maybe ... you know that Mr. Truffaut is not kidding with anyone; when it comes to money and work reputation, he does not look at who is standing in front of him; He leaves out the person who caused it; "In short, I told you to concentrate".

"Mr. Gerard's very well; thank you for reminding me. "From now on, I will concentrate more." And they got to work.

John thought again, this time thinking about what to say to Mr. Gerard! John knew that Mr. Gerard was unsatisfied with what he was saying, and perhaps a little disappointed that he did not consider him a confidant of his secrets. John, on the other hand, wanted to talk to someone to relax a little, and he knew he needed to talk to someone like Mr. Gerard to be able to use his guidance. After some thought, he decided to talk to Mr. Gerard. Of course, if there is a place where they are alone at rest; So now he just thought about his job. They were making lunch. Mr. Gerard and John had four cookbooks on their agenda each day. They prepared a varied menu of old and new French dishes and changed the menu every day, and this was accompanied by more customer attraction; Because the customer could test different flavors of food on different days. After the customers came and went and the mealtime was over, each staff member picked up his food and went to a restaurant to eat. John ate with Richard most of the time, but that day because he wanted to talk to Mr. Gerard; So he wanted to suggest to Mr. Gerard that they eat together, but before he could offer it to Mr. Gerard, Richard came to him and said, "What are you eating today, so that I can prepare for you and let you eat?"

"Excuse me, Richard," John said. But today I want to have lunch with Mr. Gerard; If possible, only today. I have word with Mr. Gerard; is it possible"?

"Okay, do as you please," said Richard, who was upset.

John noticed Richard's grief, but had no choice and said to himself that I would make it up to him later ... and went to

Mr. Gerard and said, "Mr. Gerard would you like to have lunch with me today"?

Mr. Gerard, who sometimes ate with Mr. Truffaut, decided to do the same that day, but when he saw that John had made the request, he knew from the look on his face that he wanted to tell him something; So he decided to cancel his lunch appointment with Mr. Truffaut that day and apologize to Mr. Truffaut, and said to John, "Okay, son, so bring me some food and take to the staff dining room so I can get there".

"very well," John said. If we can go somewhere that is secluded; "It's very crowded there".

"Okay," said Mr. Gerard. "Take it wherever you like".

"What do you want ?" John said.

"It does not matter," Mr. Gerard said. "Whatever you like, to your taste ... I wash my hands".

John served the food and went to a secluded place where no one was there and waited for Mr. Gerard to come and then they would eat together.

Mr. Gerard went to Mr. Truffaut and apologized for not being able to have lunch with Mr. Truffaut. Mr. Truffaut said he had no problem and could do his job. Mr. Gerard joined John and they ate.

The first minutes passed in silence; Then Mr. Gerard said, "I feel you want to tell me something; is it true"?

"Yes," said John, "you know"...

"Speak, my son," said Mr. Gerard. "Why are you so anxious"?

"You know ... I do not know where to start!" John said.

Mr. Gerard smiled and said, "Well, start from the beginning; "It's easier".

John smiled at Mr. Gerard and said, "Very well; Honestly, I lost my parents three years ago. "They were killed in a bank accident ..." and told the whole story to Mr. Gerard; Of course, he only described Rose and Stuart being killed and how he realized yesterday how they were killed, but he did not say anything about the coins or what Dallahan wanted from them.

Mr. Gerrard listened to John's story and ate as he listened, but as the story progressed, Mr. Gerrard ate less. It was as if he had lost his appetite. By the time the story was over, Mr. Gerrard had not finished eating and had stopped eating altogether. John, who had eaten nothing but the first two or three spoons

"I'm sorry I made you not eat your food," John said when he saw Mr.Gerard's surprise that caused him to give up his food and look at him lovingly.

Mr. Gerard still seemed to be amazed, looking at John and watching him without blinking. "Is there a problem, Mr. Gerard?" John asked.

Mr. Gerard came to his senses with this question, and as someone resurrected with a shock device, he blinked again, took a deep breath, and after a second said, "You see destiny!" "It looks like you and I should be in touch".

"How about Mr. Gerard?" Said, John.

"I was at the bank that day," Mr. Gerard said. I had gone to deposit money in my wife's account in France when those damn thieves came and robbed the bank, and that horrible thing happened to ... "Mr. Gerard paused and continued again:" I'm sorry, John! I'm sorry that this happened to you! That day I too - I saw how that thief treated your father; It was as if the purpose of that theft was only your father and nothing else; however, it was as if he did not think so and was taking money from the bank manager and throwing them in a bag; Anyway, what should not have happened occurred and they left. Sometime later, I followed up to see if the thieves were caught; "Unfortunately, it was as if they had melted and gone to the ground".

Mr. Gerard looked sad and said, "My son, if I can help you, tell me; "I will do whatever I can".

"Thank you, Mr. Gerard," John said. But at the moment I do not know what to do; all I know is that I want to find that person and hand over the law. "my feeling tells me that he had a personal animosity with my father and he will probably come to me sooner or later".

"He can do nothing," Mr. Gerard said. We protect you here. "Do you want me to tell the police"?

"It's useless," John said. He does not show himself soon; "I have to do something myself".

Mr. Gerard, not knowing what was right and what he should do shrugged and then stared at one point. It was as if he was thinking about that day of bank robbery; because his face looked very anxious and confused. After a moment of silence, he said, "John, you have a very great soul and heart. "I'm glad to work with you." And then he hugged and kissed John.

John was surprised; from a man as old as Mr. Gerard, it was so unlikely that he had become so emotional. Mr. Gerard left John and said, "Whatever problem you have, I will not hesitate; be sure to tell me." And then he left.

John was still sitting in the same chair, thinking about his fate and that of Dallahan, how he could trap him. It was in these thoughts that Mr. Truffaut came and said, "You do not want to go to your work"!

"Excuse me, Mr. Truffaut," John said. "Of course, I'm going".

Mr. Truffaut took a look and then went to his office to sit at his desk and count the money he had earned that day. John got up and went to work in the kitchen. From that day on, Mr. Gerard had a special respect for John and treated him differently. The rest of the people were surprised by Mr. Gerard's behavior, but they could not say anything, and it went on for several days. One day John was eating lunch when someone entered the restaurant. The light shining from the window covered the man's face and his face was not clear, but his large body was clear. Mr. Havins stepped forward and said, "Excuse me, sir! The restaurant is closed; "Lunchtime is over".

"I did not come for lunch," said the unidentified man. "I came to see Mr. Wilson".

Because everyone called John by his first name, they forgot John's family. "Mr. Wilson does not work here," Mr. Havins said.

"He said he works here," said the unidentified man.

"What's his first name?" Said Mr. Havins.

"John ... John Wilson," the man said.

"Oh," said Mr. Havins. You have word with that little boy. I must have guessed that you were John's friend. It is clear from the situation that you are dealing with him. Now is the time for lunch; He should be able to speak, but stay here until I call him. Do not move, know that I see everywhere; Do you understand boy!

Ted was not afraid of anyone, but Mr. Havins behaved strangely and said, "Okay, old man".

Mr. Havins looked at Ted and went to call John. John was sitting in the staff room eating while he was almost done when Mr. Havins called him downstairs:

"John ... John ... where are you!" hurry up, come here; "Someone has come and wants to see you; John"...

Without hesitation, John reached out to Mr. Havins so that he would not make any more noise: "Yes, Mr. Havins; "Who is dealing with me"?

Mr. Havins grumbled a little, "A big, fat boy says he has word with you." I should tell you! "You are not talking to him here".

" Very well Mr. Havins," John said. "I talk to him outside the restaurant." And then he went to the entrance of the restaurant and there he saw Ted waiting and, according to Mr. Havins' order, he did not move. It seemed that the only person Ted listened to was Mr. Havins.

John reached out to Ted and said, "How are you, Ted?" So, you finally decided to come and see me. "Are you ok friend"?

"Hello boy," Ted said. I am not bad; Yes, I came here. How are you? "Is the situation good"?

John saw that Mr. Havins was coming up the stairs, and he knew he had come to see if they were there or if they had gone out. "Let's go out and talk so that Mr. Havins is not picked on," he told to Ted.

Ted and John left the restaurant; there was a bench next to the bridge from where you could watch the sunset. John took

Ted there and they sat on that bench. Mr. Havins saw them through the window, relieved that they were not inside the restaurant, and then left.

John looked at Ted and said, "What's the matter, friend?" you look pokey! Is there a problem"?

" problem," Ted said. The problem that cannot be said is; "It's a small thing".

"Well, tell me," John said. "Maybe I can do something".

" I argued with my father again; This time, he slapped me in the ear," Ted said. I left, I came out and said I will not go back and my father, as if he was happy, told me not to go back; "My mother was crying, but my father was not paying attention."

"What happened?" Said, John. "What did you do when your father hit you"?

"Nothing," Ted said. I took my father's car without permission and hit it in a tree. I wanted to learn to drive. Oh, every time I told my father to teach me to drive, he would say, it is soon and you will learn at the time. I do not know; I have to rip to be able to drive! Am I a fruit?! With this body, both my foot gets to the pedal and my mind gets to know how to drive. I recently found out that I am very interested in cars and driving. My father and I had been going to the garage for a few days to repair a car. I was doing well; my father was happy with me. Well, I did not think I would hit the tree. Oh, a kitten came forward; I turned the handlebar so as not to hit it; suddenly I did not understand what happened when that tree appeared in front of me. Fat chance! I always have to bring bad luck somewhere! "I cannot be on the routine"!

John put his hand on his friend's back and said, "Do not worry, comrade; That's right. Your father is angry now; be sure to say something like that; "Whatever it is, you are his son".

"Don't worry," Ted said. This is not the first time I have left the house. Honestly, I do not want to worry my mother. Well let this go; tell me, what's new? What did you do? Tell the truth; what did you do with that pot? Trick...! I could not believe that day that you took that pot as a souvenir ... oh, how you have not been looking for it for so many years! Ha ? "

When John saw that he could not deceive Ted, he said, "Honestly, in that pot, it was a safe deposit key that my mother put in the bank for me; I took that key and ... "And he told the rest of the story of the bank to Ted, what the bank officer said and gave the details of the thief, and that he decided to look for the thief and find the thief. After John's story was over, Ted said to John, "Hey friend! Know that I am with you until the end; I used to have no excuse to leave the house, but now I know why I have to leave. Whenever you're ready and want to move, tell me. Until then, I will provide the necessary equipment and equip ourselves so that there is no problem.

John regretted telling this story to Ted; He did not think that Ted wanted to go with him and did not know what to say to dissuade him ...: "Oh, Ted it is not possible. Your mother is waiting for you; "You can't come with me".

Ted said firmly, "Oh, here is no ifs or buts; I come; Just what I said. I cannot let you go to find this thief alone. You've been alone enough for a few years and I did not come looking for you, but from now on it will be different; be sure you need help along the way. I do not know where you want to go, but wherever you want, it does not matter; "I am ready to go to the farthest point".

"Oh, Ted ... This way, we can't do it," John said. "In this way, tell me in advance that I will come and I will accept"!

"I do not want to hear anything about it anymore," Ted said. As I said; it's over. It is not up to you to accept. Do not you remember when we were children; your father always handed you over to me and told me to take care of you? I'm doing what your father said. "Do you want me to ignore your father's words?"

John had no choice but to accept. A few minutes passed without talking or staring at the sunset. And they enjoyed seeing that beautiful sunset. At that moment, Richard came out of the restaurant and reached himself to Ted and John, saying, "John! John!" where are you? I searched you everywhere until Mr. Havins finally told me that you sit here. Mr. Gerard was searching for you; He told me to call for help. "It's been an hour now from the rest time".

"Wow ... It's too late," John said. We talked so much that we did not notice the passage of time. I forgot to introduce "This is my friend Ted and Ted, this is my friend Richard".

Richard smiled and held out his hand. "I'm glad to meet you." Ted took Richard by the hand and said, "Me too".

"All right, Ted, I have to go," John said. It's too late. "If so, we will meet again next week and talk in detail." "Okay," Ted said. Just be careful don't leave me; "Because I will keep eye on you!" "No, Ted, we'll talk later," John smiled and said. He glanced at Richard, and Ted noticed, "Very well."

Bye. Take care. Let me know if you have a problem. Goodbye for now".

"Thank you, Ted," John said. "Say hello to your mother and tell her I miss the cookies she made".

"Okay, John," Ted said. "I tell her." And he said goodbye and left. John and Richard also went to the restaurant. "I had not seen this friend of yours during this time," said Richard.

"Yeah," said John, "Ted was a childhood friend; "He is a good boy".

"You mean you are the same age?" Richard said? He is much older! He seems to be older than me; How interesting!" Then they entered the restaurant and John went to the kitchen. On the way to the kitchen, he saw Mr. Havins waiting for John to come and start grunting. And John knew it. After Mr. Havins' grunts were over, John went to the kitchen and saw that Mr. Gerard was waiting for him; so he apologized to Mr. Gerard and explained Ted's case to him, and then they got to work.

It's been almost a month since John's last leave, and John was able to take leave again. This time he took leave only in the afternoon and went to Ted without the opposition of Mr. Truffaut and Gerard. After the doorbell rang, a kind woman of medium height, slightly flat, and dark curly brown hair opened the door and said, "Yes ... did you have anything to do, son?" "If you have word with Ted, he's not home".

"Are you okay, Mrs. Baggins?" Said, John. I'm John ... John Wilson. "Oh, how I wished to see you".

"Oh, oh John," said Mrs. Baggins. "Ever since Ted told me about it, I told him to bring you here one day to see you." And then he hugged John and continued: "Well, why are you waiting! Come on in, sit down until Ted arrives. He has gone somewhere; "He will be back soon".

John came in and sat down on a chair. Mrs. Baggins went to the kitchen to get something for John. A few minutes later, he returned with a cup of coffee and some cookies and said, "Ted told me that you like my cookies very much."Well, you were lucky that I made cookies today, and it was as if you smelled the cookies and came here".

"Yes, Mrs. Baggins, I have loved and enjoyed your cookies since I was a child, and it was my good fortune to be here today," John smiled and said.

"Yes, my son, eat," said Mrs. Baggins. Enjoy it." And then he sat down on the sofa with John and took a deep breath and said, "Ted told me the story of your life and said that you have suffered a lot during this time; sorry I could not bring you here after your grandmother died!"I love you as much as Ted."

"Thank you, Mrs. Baggins, but I'm not upset with you," John said. John was eating coffee and cookies and enjoying it when the doorbell rang. Mrs. Baggins went and opened the door, and Ted entered with various tools. Seeing John, a smile settled on his lips and he said, "Hello John. How're you? Finally, you came ... I'm going to leave this in my room; "I'm coming back".

John greeted Ted and said, "Okay, Ted. "I am sitting here for you to come".

Ted returned a few minutes later and sat down next to John and said to his mother, "Mom, can you bring something to eat?" "Yes, my son, I will," Baggins said "I always have food for you." Mrs. Baggins said these things with special affection. It turned out that he loved Ted very much. "Well ...what!" Said Ted as Mrs. Baggins prepared food for Ted. What did you do, John? Do you know where we should go? I prepared things for this one week and these things that you saw today were for traveling. "Now, after eating, we will go to my room to see them and we will talk".

"Okay, Ted," John said. But you told your mother you wanted to come with me? "And your mother allowed it"?

"Are you crazy?" Ted said. If I tell her that she will not let me leave the house. The day we wanted to leave; I'll say it. "At that time, even if she objects, it is not a problem".

Please show mercy to her.," John said, "you want to leave and come with me to an unknown path"!

"Don't worry about these things," Ted said. "Eat your cookies".

At that moment, Mrs. Baggins came and placed a meal in front of Ted and said, "Tonight, in honor of John, I want to make a delicious meal; "We have a great guest".

"How good it is," Ted said as he ate, holding a bite in his mouth. "So, I tell John to come to our house every night".

Mrs. Baggins smiled and said, of course, he will be welcome." And then she went to the kitchen to prepare dinner.

After eating, Ted and John went to Ted's room to talk about their trip and to see what Ted had taken. Over the past week, John has thought about where to look for the Dallahan and has concluded that if they go looking for the coins, the

Dallahan will show himself and they must be prepared for that moment. John decided to tell the whole story to Ted; In any case, Ted is willing to risk his life for his sake; so he has a right to know everything and why his parents were killed. When they got to Ted's room, they first checked the equipment. Ted had bought various items; He even bought a traveling tent and other items needed for the trip.

"I used to go camping on behalf of the school in the summer," Ted said. That's why I almost knew what we needed and I prepared these; "I hope it is enough and there will be no problem."

John was happy to see that scene and those devices; that he has a companion like Ted and can trust him; that he no longer felt lonely. John thanked Ted and said, "Ted, I want to tell you some facts; "Are you ready to hear it"?

"You mean worse than that bank story?" Ted said.

"Yeah Ted, I think it's worse," John said.

"Boy, why is your life so full of mysteries?" Ted said. So, tell me what else! Let me just tell you that whatever it is, we will go on this journey together; OK"?

John accepted and prepared to tell his life story; this was the first time he wanted to explain it to someone, completely.

John told his story from the beginning; From the magic dumpster and that mysterious alley and that black object and the letter ... and all that had happened and Ted should have known to come to this journey with awareness. John told the whole story. It's been almost two hours since he finished his speech. Ted was confused again; He sat on the bed for ten minutes in silence and thought, thinking of John's words, and then said to John, "Now I am more determined than ever to come to you; not for those coins; because this coward has taken your parents away from you twice. I'm sure God wants you to find him; otherwise, you would not have found that dumpster and that alley. It all depends on your decision when you want to move; "Because whenever you say that, I'm ready to go".

John was very happy to have a good friend like Ted. He felt that he did not regret explaining everything to Ted, and Ted answered his trust. "Thank you, my friend," he said to Ted. You fill the void of my parents for me; "I hope I can respond to your kindness".

"What a joke," Ted said. "Friendship is useful these days".

It was during this conversation that Mrs. Baggins knocked on the door several times and said, "Ted, the food is ready."

Ted opened the door and his mother said, "Your father has come".

Ted turned and said, "My father has come; "Let's go, John, to introduce you to him." My father always liked you; because you were a kid who always dreamed. Let's go." And they both went to the kitchen. Mr. Baggins was sitting there waiting for food to be brought. When he saw Ted and John, he said, "Hello, guys. "Ted, do not you want to introduce your friend to me"?

Ted was amazed at his father's mood, which was good for him, and he said, "Yes, father, John Wilson, "John who lived in the building on the other side".

"Hello, Mr. Baggins," John said. Nice to meet you. "Thank you for accepting me." And he stretched out his hand, and Mr. Baggins shook his hand gently, saying, "You have been so polite since childhood; even after all these years and hardships, you still have politeness. Well done my son! Well done! ¬ I wish all of Ted's friends were like you! ¬ »and looked sharply at Ted. Ted was relieved to find that his father had the same mood as before, and spoke well with him only to maintain his appearance, and said, "Yes, father, from now on, I am only with my friend John; I have nothing to do with the rest of my friends anymore. "I drew a line around them all."

Ted's father was delighted to hear this and said, "I'm glad John is back to bring you back to life".

"Very well," said Mrs. Baggins. Leave the table alone. "You two should wash your hands and get ready for dinner".

John and Ted washed their hands and returned. Mrs. Baggins also set the table. The smell of food was everywhere. John missed his mother. He had not been in a family gathering for a long time. Everyone was eating; When John ate the first bite, the food reminded him of all his childhood memories, so tears welled up in his eyes. Seeing that scene, Ted said, "Don't be emotional, boy! An ordinary meal. "If you promise to be a good kid, you will come once a week to eat this food".

John smiled and said that he remembered the old days and his parents. That night went well and John was about to return to the restaurant. It was about eleven o'clock and John was about to leave when Mr. Baggins said, "Wait; "Let me take you".

"I'm coming too," said Ted, happy with his father. And they went together and took John to the restaurant.

That night, John did not sleep and spent the whole night thinking about the journey and how to go about it. Decided to read the letter; Maybe he will find something new other than what his father had understood from the letter. He went to the black object, took the letter out of its place and opened it, and began to read the letter with a little anxiety. The letter referred to the place where his father had gone, but inside the letter was a part that was not in French and it was not clear in what language it was written. His father had also drawn the red line below that part, and it was clear that he had not noticed anything, so his father was sure that there must be another place for these coins. John tried very hard to figure out what the illegible part was written in. The type of script seemed too old; because it did not look like any other script in the world. John decided to look at different old scripts so that he might find a resemblance between this script and the old version and decided to go to the city's central library tomorrow. He was sure he would find something about that script there; so, he put the letter in its place and that item in the closet. As he placed the black object in the cupboard, his eyes fell on the gifts in the dumpster; He picked up the Binoculars and sat down on the bed, playing with the Binoculars a little while he was thinking, opening, and closing it regularly. He said to himself, I wish I could see where my father went and know what a place it is to be fully prepared. I wish my father had told my mother more memories of that place so that I would know how to get there. Wow, what if it happened! After coming out of these thoughts and seeing the Binoculars in his hand playing with it, he remembered what he had taken the Binoculars for and wanted to see outside with it, but because of the darkness, he gave up, but he has tempted again and said to himself that now it is not harmful to try it and he picked up the Binoculars again and opened it and went to the window. He opened the window to see better outside and brought the Binoculars closer to his eyes. To his surprise, he saw a landscape that looked like a forest. He took the Binoculars out of the front of his eyes and whispered, "It is not possible!" That's what I saw! He put the Binoculars in front of his eyes again and looked carefully; and saw the same place again. He lowered the Binoculars quickly and looked at the other side of the Binoculars so that if anything stuck to it, he would pick it up; but it was nothing but a lens! He could not believe it! Although it had happened to him before, he still had a hard time believing it. He looked at the Binoculars again. The question for him was what is this image? This time he held the Binoculars up and turned it slightly; He was surprised to see that the image also moved by rotating the Binoculars.

John lowered the Binoculars in astonishment and sat on the bed to feel a little better. He wondered what image he was seeing! After a while, he thought to himself, "Well, what was I thinking?" The place my father went to ... Well, maybe this is the place! Maybe this Binocular only shows there. The treasure hiding place must be related to the image that the dumpster gave me these Binoculars. So far, everything I got from there has been about my family ... yes, it certainly is ... yes, that's right; Otherwise, I would not have been given this Binocular. So now how do I find the treasure in the picture? I wish I knew where my father went! I wish Ted was here now to talk to him a little! I was getting calmer. If it could, it would be great, but it's a pity he's not here. He picked up the Binoculars again to see the scene again, but this time when he put the camera in front of his eyes, he was surprised to see another image! He saw Ted sitting in his room, packing up the things he had bought. He almost screamed in surprise, but he closed his mouth. Then he sat down and said to himself, I think I understood how to work with this Binocular... Whatever I think, the Binoculars show the same place. This is great; great! It was as if the dumpster knew what I needed and gave me these Binoculars.

John was very happy to have such a thing. It was a wonderful gift. He was sitting on the bed, thinking ... he remembered another camera; that camera certainly has a special function. That camera should work, too. Then he happily picked it up and took a picture from one point. But it was a real photo, and the photo he took was no different from the subject; he said to him, "Well, I must think of something." John thought of their old house and took a picture of the outside view, but it was still a real picture, and the picture he took was the same dark view outside. John thought, well, this is probably just a regular camera for capturing moments, and he put both camera and Binoculars in the closet. He turned off the light and went into his bed. He decided to go to Ted tomorrow and talk to him about the Binoculars; also, to go to the library to get information about that special script; so went to bed early.

John fell asleep and saw Rose and her mother Emily sitting in the yard talking. Her mother looked like the picture he had at the same age and Rose was younger than the time he remembered. They were drinking tea when François entered with a tall man with a ponytail and black hair and curly beard and small, light brown eyes. Emily seemed to know him; because he greeted him warmly. Rose greeted him and then got up and went to her house and they sat there. Emily brought coffee for François and the man, and they started drinking coffee and talking warmly. That scene was over and

John saw a new scene again; This time, his father and the man were in the train wagon; His father looked a little older; It was probably a few years later, and they were sitting in the same wagon talking, that a man of medium height and with stubble entered the wagon and asked them to sit in that cart, and his father allowed him, but the man who seemed to be his father's friend was unhappy with the man sitting in the cart, and John saw nothing.

 He woke up at about six in the morning. He thought of the dream he had. From last night until that hour, many strange things had happened to him; everything was very strange. He did not know in which direction he would be drawn, but he knew that a force was protecting him, and he was sure that if he entered this way, he would not be harmed, and that force would take care of him. He took a deep breath and got up to wash his hands and face. John did not know how to get Mr. Truffaut permission to go out. It was the 23rd of August and there was nothing left at the end of the month. John decided not to work in the restaurant from the beginning of the month and to travel; Of course, if his travel route has been determined by then. So, he did not want to leave at that time and had to work there to have a place to sleep. He worked until noon that day and went to Mr. Truffaut with great stress to get permission, but he was not there. He asked Mr. Havins about Mr. Truffaut, and Mr. Havns said he did not come today, and told him to tell Mr. Gerard if he had anything to do. John was glad Mr. Truffaut was gone; because he did not have to ask his permission, he went to Mr. Gerard, who was in the kitchen, as usual, cooking for himself to go to the staff room. John reached out to him and said: "Excuse me, Mr. Gerard! I had a request; "Of course, if possible." "What, my son?" Said Mr. Gerard. "Do you want to take leave again"?

"Yes, Mr. Gerard," John said; if it's possible? "Vacation is about the same thing, you know."

"Well, You have chosen a good time," Mr. Gerard said. Neither is Mr. Truffaut. Okay, no problem, but try not to let Mr. Havins know you're leaving; because if he finds out, he will tell Mr. Truffaut that I do not think he will agree with you leaving; so, it's better to go quietly and come back. "Of course, tell Richard to open the door for you at night".

" of course Mr. Gerard's; Sure," John said and he thanked Mr. Gerard and went to talk to Richard. Richard was eating in the staff room; John ate his food and sat down next to Richard. Richard was delighted to see John and said, "Good! "Why did you come to me and eat with me?" "Don't say that old friend Richard ..." John said, then continued, "I wanted to say something." And then he lowered his voice and continued, "I want to go out. Mr. Gerard knows, but I do not want Mr. Havins to know; "Because he tells Mr. Truffaut and he gets upset".

"Where do you want to go this time?" Richard said. "Are you tired of that amusement park"?

"What are you talking about?" John said. I will not go there; I have word with Ted. "Did you see Ted"?

"Yes, I saw him," Richard said. Yeah well ... that's an older friend; "you have to spend time with him".

"Oh, Richard," John said. I come at night and I tell you everything that has happened to me so many times that you get rid of doubts; Do not talk about this anymore; I just ask that Mr. Havins not be aware of my absence today and open the door for me the night I come. I will be grateful. "Richard, I promise to explain everything tonight".

"I know you don't explain it, but it's okay," Richard said. I accept it because of our old friendship; "You know you should not come later than eleven o'clock".

"Yeah, Richard, I know," John said. Thank you for accepting. "I promise to say you and reciprocate this love".

He left the restaurant without anyone noticing that John was leaving. Since John only worked with Mr. Gerard, no one noticed him. The only person who cared a lot about the people in the kitchen was Mr. Havins, especially since Mr. Truffaut was not there that day and Mr. Havins had his eye on the restaurant, but Mr. Gerard had told John that he was doing something that Mr. Havins would not notice. And whenever Mr. Havins asked about John, Mr. Gerard would say that he had sent him to prepare food or that he had gone somewhere else; Of course, Mr. Havins was also a little skeptical.

After leaving the restaurant, John first decided to go to the library and find the script in the letter and, if possible, interprets it. So, he went to the central library of the city, and after arriving, he went to the old books and the books about the old manuscripts. He took a book off the shelf and began to read. He first wrote down the sentence on a piece of paper, similar to what was in the letter, so that he would not have to take the letter out of his pocket so that the letter would not be damaged.

An old man was sitting in that part of the library studying. One seemed literate. The book in the old man's hand was a collection of old manuscripts; John walked over to the old man, ignoring him, but sat down on the bench, but the old man was curious when he saw a young boy, John, studying in that part of the library. After several hours of reading, John realized that he did not understand any of those sentences. At that moment he felt someone standing over his head; when he raised his head, he saw the old man above his head. He got up and said hello. The old man smiled and shook his head in greeting, saying, "What happened, my son?" "What are you looking for in these books that have confused you so much?"

John wondered if he should tell the old man the subject of the letter. He did not know what was written there. It may be important, but he finally decided to talk to the old man so that he might understand the subject of the letter; that is why he said: "Excuse me, sir! I have a text that I think is from the Old Testament; His handwriting seems to be very old. I want to translate it; "That's why I came here and picked up this book so that maybe with the help of these books I can find the meaning of these sentences".

The old man smiled and said, "My son!"Can I see that words"?

"Yes, can you help me?" John said.

"I do not know, my son," said the old man. "I have to see what language that writing is in and for what period, so I can say whether it can be interpreted or not".

"Oh ... yes, sir," John said.

"Professor Richard Baxter," said the old man.

"Yes," said John. Well, professor. Here you are! "This is also written".

Professor Baxter took the note, looked at it as carefully as possible, and said, "From what did you take note of this"?

"I took it from an old book, which was all in French, but it was in that language and I could not read it," John said.

"You can speak French," said Professor Baxter.

"Yes," said John, "then the professor asked John in French that was he from French." And John replied that he was from New York.

The professor liked John and said, "If I could see the original text, it would be much better; But there is something that can be done about it. Let me see what happens, and then he went to a shelf of old books and from the top of those books, pulled out a book and came back and said, "I think this language belongs to ancient times, and this sentence was written in ancient Egyptian. Now I do not know what this sentence did in the middle of a French text! Anyway, I don't care; The important thing is to translate this text now. Okay; Let me see where it is ... Yes, I think I found the word I wanted to know the meaning of. Yes, I guessed right. It's an island, but my son, you have to give me time to find the rest of the words. It takes some time to put these words together; That's why I have to take the time to work on this sentence more; In particular, my specialty is not the language of ancient Egypt; "Otherwise I would be doing this for you right now".

"How long do you think you need to translate this?" John asked.

The professor replied, "why my son?" Are you in a hurry? do you have work? If you want you can go; I'm here. I have no other place to work today and I am busy in the library. You can go and come back in two to three hours. "I think by then the work of translating this text has been completed".

"Thank you very much, Professor," John said. Honestly, I do not have much time. Because I have to go somewhere and then go back to work. So, I go and come back in three hours. "Thank you, Professor."

The professor smiled at John in response and then re-examined the text, and when John saw that was doing the translation work, he went out of the library to see Ted. First of all, to find out if Ted is home or not, he decided to see it with the Binoculars; On the other hand, he could try it again. So, he took the camera out of his bag and opened it, and in his mind, he asked the Binoculars to show Ted's room; He saw Ted in his room. Even though he had seen the Binoculars work before, he was still surprised. And he moved to Ted's house. The library was not far from Ted's house; so, after a five-minute walk, he got there and pressed the bell chassis.

Mrs. Baggins opened the door as usual, and when she saw John, she said happily, "Oh ... John! That's you? Welcome my son. Come in." Then he said loudly, "Ted, come ... come; "John is here".

The next moment, the sound of a wooden floor was heard, indicating that Ted was hurrying to the front door. Ted greeted John and said, "Why are you standing?"Let's go to my room, I have word with you" said Mrs. Baggins as they tried to enter Ted's room. Take these coffees and cookies. "John loves it".

John thanked Mrs. Baggins, and Ted grabbed a tray of tea and cookies and went to his room. When they entered the room, Ted closed the door without hesitation and told John to sit down, and John sat down on the bed, and Ted began, "Today I did a little research on where we should go; "About that man ... did you say what his name was"?

"Dallahan," John said.

Ted continued, "Yeah, Dallahan, that fellow, I did some research. See if anyone knows him? I know a few guys knowing about that, but I asked everyone, no one knew the person you described. I do not know! Maybe that man did not belong to this city; otherwise, these guys will surely know him; Anyway, I packed my bags and packed as you can see. I am fully prepared; "All you have to do is tell us to move".

John was looking carefully at Ted, who was right; He was ready to travel in every way. He was a good friend. "Come sit down," John said. I want to say something. "I do not have much time; I have to go".

"Where?" Ted said. "There is still a lot of time until night".

"Come and sit down," John said. "I will explain to you".

Ted sat down in front of John, in a chair by the window, and John talked. John told what happened last night; He spoke about the Binoculars and the text of the letter, and that Professor Baxter was translating it. The more John said the more Ted was surprised. After John finished talking, Ted said, "Give me the Binoculars and let me see how it works!" And he gave the Binoculars to Ted. Without thinking, Ted put the Binoculars over his eyes and looked, but saw nothing but black, and then lowered the camera and said, "It shows nothing"!

"Have you thought of anything?" John said. "Think about where you want to see it."

"You're right," Ted said. "Well, I want to ... now see what my father does in mechanics." And then he put the Binoculars in front of his eyes, but he saw nothing but the wall, and then he threw the Binoculars at John and John took it in the air and said, "What happened?"Why did you throw it this way"?

"Did you kid me?" Ted said. That is like all Binoculars. It does not do anything special. "Do not lie about what you say!" Ted, who turned out to be upset and thought John had joked, went back to his chair and turned his face to the window.

"Ted, I'm not lying," John said. "Have I ever lied to you"?

"It was in childhood," Ted said, "but I have not seen you since." I do not know! "Maybe you lied too".

"Ted, I'm not lying," John said, upset. "I do not know why it does not work." And then he imagined the restaurant in his mind and put the Binoculars in front of his eyes and saw the picture of the restaurant and then he turned to Ted and said, "It works".

"I saw nothing," Ted said.

"Wait, maybe this just works for me," John said. "Because the dumpster gave me this Binocular." And then he said, "Ted, please go to that room, to your mother and do something, and when you come back, I'll tell you what you did".

"What's up," Ted said. Do you mock me again? Come on; I can't."

"Ted, please do it once," John said. "I promise you I'm right".

Ted looked at John, then got up reluctantly and went to the kitchen to pick up some cookies and eat them, then drink a glass of milk and return to John a few minutes later. When he returned, he said to John, "Well ... now what!"What do you want to do"?

"You went there, ate a cookie, and poured yourself a glass of milk," John said. It's true"?

"Well, what!" Said Ted.

Ted, who was more convinced, was slowly believing and said to John, "If you are right, tell me where my father is now and what he is doing.

John picked up the Binoculars and looked at the mechanic with it; but he did not see Ted's father there, and said to Ted, "Your father is not there; "It's like he's out".

Ted went to his mother and asked her mother about his father. And his mother said that he did not go to a mechanic today and had a job somewhere. Ted was still a little pleased, but still not quite convinced; so, he said, "Tell me, my friend, Taylor, what is he doing in his room?" John explained to him and Ted called his friend; John's words were right and the Binoculars were working ... he finally accepted, but he was still upset that he could not use that Binoculars, and then he said, "All right, I accepted ... OK; "Now tell us what to do".

"Professor Baxter has to translate that text first so we can see where our destination is," John said.

"Very well," Ted said. Why are you procrastinating?! Eat your coffee and cookies quickly so that if you do not eat, my mother will not let us leave the house. "Then we go to the professor."

John laughed and ate his coffee and cookies and headed for the library. After a short walk, they reached the library. On the way, they talked about the equipment they had prepared for the trip and what they should do on the trip. It had been almost three hours since John had left the library. They both entered the library. Professor Baxter was still working on the text, immersed in the book. When they reached the professor, the professor did not notice at all. John cleared his throat a little; the professor looked at them and said, "Oh ... you are my son! It passed so soon! Three hours over? Oh ... but I've not finished this text yet; There are still some words that I did not find the meaning of, and without those words, the text would not have a clear meaning. Sorry, my son! I did not think it would be so difficult, but I promise to make sense of it anyway. I have a friend who is a teacher of this language and I think he can help us. Unfortunately, he is not in New York today and has gone to Chicago to attend the conference. We have to wait for him to come. Until then, I am still working on this text. If I could make sense, I would let you know. Where can I find you? John gave the address of the restaurant. The professor had seen Ted and said, "Oh ... I'm sorry! I just saw you; "I did not notice at all".

"There is nothing wrong, Professor," Ted said. "I think you paid so much attention to this text that you did not see me with this body".

The professor smiled and said to John, "I think Professor Taylor is coming to New York tomorrow, and I'll text him to call me." Whenever the work of translating this text is finished, I will come to you. "When I get there, tell them who I want to see?"

"I'm John Wilson, Professor," John said.

"I'm glad to meet you, dear John," said Professor Baxter. "Everything will be fine, my son." Then he put his hand in his pocket and handed him a card, saying, "My son; this is my card. If you have something to do, call this number. I am very happy to see a boy your age reading such a text, and I remembered my youth. Good luck." And after that, he said goodbye to John and Ted and left. John and Ted also came out of the library. John glanced at the library clock; it was about 9:30. "I have to go," John said. I should not be late. "Mr. Havins should not understand that I was not there."

"Okay, John," Ted said. Take care. If there is news, let me know; Well boy …"

"Okay, Ted, I'll tell you," John said. Take care of yourself too; Goodbye for now".

Ted and John parted, and Ted headed home and John headed to the restaurant. John felt again that someone was seeing him from a distance, but he could not understand who he was. When he arrived at the restaurant, Mr. Gerard was still there and almost no customer. When he arrived, Richard opened the door and said, "Mr. Havins is in the kitchen, and I think he's still looking for you."

Richard had brought John's clothes with him. John took them and changed them and went down the stairs. When he got to the kitchen, Mr. Havins was behind the staircase, walking around the end of the hall. It was as if he was looking for John. Mr. Gerard saw John and asked him to come with him, and John hurried there. After searching, Mr. Havins came back to Mr. Gerard and saw John and said, "What a surprise! We saw you. You were so much here and there today! Be careful with your job, John. "You know I take care of everything." And looked at John angrily...

"Of course Mr. Havins," John said. "But I was following Mr. Gerard's orders".

"Yes, Mr. Gerard said where you were," Mr. Havins said, glancing at Mr. Gerrard.? 'Be careful about your job boy, and went up the stairs to the hall to check on it. "You were too late," Mr. Gerard told John after Mr. Havins left. It's as if Mr. Havins had a mission today to just check this part. So ... what happened? Did you do your job? Were you able to conclude? "Did you find a clue from that person?"

"Not yet, but I got a little closer," John said. "I think I can get good news in a few days".

" I hope you succeed," Mr. Gerard said. Now go and get some food for yourself. You're pale as death; I think you have not eaten since morning. Go my son; "I did the work myself".

John thanked Mr. Gerard, and since he was very hungry, he ate his food and ate in the same kitchen. The next day, John spent the whole day thinking about Professor Baxter, and everyone who came in the door waited for him to be found, but there was no news. Decided to see Professor with the Binoculars who was able to talk to Professor Taylor? So, he thought of the address on the back of Professor Baxter's business card, put the Binoculars in front of his eyes, and saw the professor's room. No one was there and the room was empty. John thought it best to wait until tomorrow. If there is no news from the professor, he would call him later; so lie down and sleep. John had been waiting for Professor Baxter again since morning; after lunchtime was over, John's patience has been tried; That's why he called the professor. Nobody picked up the phone. John did not know what had happened. Was the professor able to translate the text or not? He decided to go to his room and see the professor's room with the Binoculars, but he did not see anyone. He saw the library again with the Binoculars; Looked at the same place he had seen the professor before; He saw the professor sitting with a man talking about a difficult subject. John guesses that person must be Professor Taylor. And they were probably talking about that text. John would have loved to go to the library and find out the result, but he could not; Because Mr. Truffaut was there and could not tell Ted. He was afraid Ted would make things worse; anyway, that day is over. John did not pay attention at all, and Mr. Gerard realized this, but he did not take it too hard because he knew that John was involved in something important.

At night, when he went to his room, he looked at the library with the Binoculars; No one was there. Then he saw Professor Baxter's room; Professors Baxter and Taylor were there, and it was clear they were focused on something. John immediately went out to contact Professor Baxter's office.

He went to the counter in front of the restaurant and dialed Mr. Baxter; after a few beeps, he heard Professor Baxter say, "Hello, Professor. I'm John. I wanted to talk to you about that text. "Did you conclude?"

"Are you John?" Said Professor Baxter. Yes, we got good results. There are only two or three words left that I think will be finished by tomorrow. If you can, come to the library tomorrow at noon. "I think I can take it to you."

John was happy and thanked the professor and said that he would come there tomorrow at break time, and he hung up the phone and went to his room. He slept peacefully that night.

The next morning, John woke up and started working on his aperture, but his eyes were on the clock all the time. Moments passed very slowly for John. Finally, after work and a break, John quickly changed his work clothes and went to the library without eating lunch. He wanted to return soon so as not to use Mr. Truffaut as an excuse; so he told Mr. Gerard and he left quickly. John ran all the way to get there sooner. When he got to the library, Professor Baxter was sitting there studying. The translation of the text seemed to be over; John greeted him, and Professor Baxter raised his head and said, "Hello John. How are you, my son? You came looking for that special text. Ah ... let me see where I put it ... it was here. I think I put it next to the book. "Give me a chance." And then he took the book out of the bag and opened the special pages that he had already marked, and took out a piece of paper and gave it to him. John took the paper and said, "I do not know how to repay your compliment"!

"As I was able to translate this text, I enjoyed it," said Professor Baxter. I like to flip through old texts and I do not mind at all; it is also fun. "I hope you get what you want, and this text can help".

"So," John said. I hope I can repay your great grace in the future. Excuse me, I'm in a hurry; my rest time is coming to an end; I have to go back to work. "I would love to see you again, Professor".

"I would also like to see you and know where you are going with this text," said Professor Baxter. My office is always open to you. I'm there whenever you want; "Take care of yourself, son".

John said goodbye to Professor Baxter and left the library and went to the restaurant. There were still a few minutes left until the end of the rest hour; so, he went to eat something and put that text in the cupboard so that he could read it later.

It was night and it arrived when John was waiting for. After finishing his work, John went to the bathroom to read the text more calmly and focused. Then he came to his room and sat on the bed and took the letter out of the closet and began to read the letter.

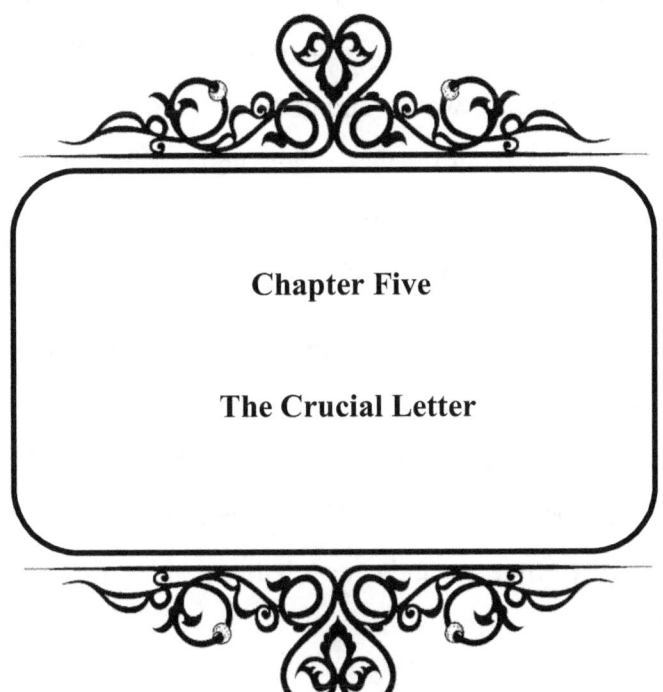

Chapter Five

The Crucial Letter

"O you who are one of my descendants and you read this letter, know that what you are looking for will be found in the islands underwater. Return to your hometown and there you will find an island surrounded by mountains and dual black rocks; Blue and colorful water; an island with a variety of colors; O child, know that this is the place you want. In the southeast of the island, where the soil is different, go to the sea in the blue waters and go twenty miles away from the island and go under the water there and next to the huge rock you will find what you are waiting for; " you May use what I have left for you properly".

John read the letter several times to understand the text of the letter correctly. John wondered if Professor Baxter should be curious as to what was hidden by reading this letter and john became anxious. He decided to talk to Ted about the island tomorrow and research the island to find out where it was.

When he woke up in the morning, he informed Ted and asked him to research the island and see which of the French islands resembled these characteristics. While working with Mr. Gerard, he talked about the French islands and which of the French islands is more beautiful. John spoke cleverly of the island so that when Mr. Gerard could speak of the French islands, John would know which one was closer. Mr. Gerard said that the island of Bora Bora is one of the most beautiful islands in France, where the people of Haiti work in agriculture. There are various fruits such as bananas, coconuts, and fruits similar to tropical fruits. The island is surrounded by three colors: green, turquoise, and dark blue. "If you go to France one day, be sure to visit this island," he told John. Because it is so beautiful, colorful island with many divers. John thought that the island he was looking for should be this one; because he was close to the specifications of that letter, he was worried, of course, that despite the divers who were there, they might have found that treasure till now, or maybe ... John's mind was full of these possibilities and ifs. John thought that I should go there anyway to find out if there was a treasure. I do not think I will lose anything. I will go on a journey later and look for that treasure. John was so engrossed in his thoughts that Mr. Gerard said, "It is as if, with these definitions, I have made of Bora Bora Island, you have imagined yourself there, and you are drowning in your dreams!" And laughed.

"Yeah, Mr. Gerard, I thought I was imagining myself there," said John, embarrassed, afraid that Mr. Gerard would find out. It must be a beautiful place. "If I want to go to France one day, I will go there".

It was time for lunch the next day; John was eating when Mr. Havins came down and approached John with the same grunt he had always said. "Get up, boy!" The same annoying boy has come again and is dealing with you. Go and come back soon; I do want to see that you will be late this time either ... You are also talking outside of here. "Did you understand?"

"Yes, Mr. Havins, thank you," John said and moved to the entrance. Ted was waiting for John in the same place as before; He was sitting on a bench in front of the sea. When John came, Ted got up and shook his hand.

"What's up," John said. What did you do? "Where did the investigation go"?

Ted smiled and said, "How hurried! Wait, I will say one by one. Come sit here first; "I will explain to you".

John sat down on the bench next to Ted and said, "Well! Start; I am waiting".

"According to my research, the only island that was very similar to the one you described is Bora Bora," Ted said. The photo I saw of this island has similar characteristics, but it is a bit expensive to travel there. "We hope to be able to pay for this trip".

"Don't think about it," John said. I saved some money. "I think we should go there".

"Really," Ted said. Let me read the full text of the letter. "John gave the translation of that letter to Ted".

"Now how can we go underwater?" Ted said. We do not know how to dive and we do not have anyone who can be trusted. To get there, you must be a professional diver; "Because, as the letter says, we must go to the bottom of the water to get it out".

"I can't think of anything right now, I don't know what to do," John said. I did not think I had to go underwater to find that treasure. The situation is a bit complicated; "I just hope that what we find is worth all the hard work." John got up and continued, "I have to think I can find a solution! Go now. I will return to work too. Rest time is over. We are in touch; I'll keep you informed".

"Okay, John," Ted said. "I'm researching to see if I can do something."

John said goodbye to Ted and John went to the restaurant and got to work. John's business hours were over and all the customers were gone. Richard was cleaning the hall, and John went to his room to rest and think about the island after he had finished his work and Mr. Gerard was gone. He decided to talk to Ted tomorrow afternoon about it.

It was morning, and John asked Mr. Truffaut permission to visit his friend; Although Mr. Truffaut grumbled, he accepted. John had decided to take his camera with him. Maybe it works and maybe he wants to take a picture of something; so he put them in his bag. Before going to Ted, he saw him with the camera sitting at home, working on the computer. After making sure he was home, he walked over to him.

When he got there, Ted's mother greeted him warmly as usual and invited John inside. Before Ted came out, John went to his room and entered the room. Ted was working on the computer as John had seen.

"Hello," John said. What did you do? "Were you able to find a solution"?

"Hello," Ted said. "No, what about you"?

"No, I have not thought of anything yet," John said. We must know how to get to that part of the sea before leaving. "Were you able to determine how to get there"? Is the path clear?

"Yeah," Ted said, "from here we have to go to Paris, and from there to Pierrelate Airport in Tahiti, and from there to

Bora Bora Airport, and from there to the hotel we booked earlier; Just as easily. "The main part of the trip is going to the sea and diving there".

"Yeah, I don't know what to do," John said. "I wish I could get help from Mr. Gerard, but it might be difficult".

John and Ted searched for information about Bora Bora Island. A few hours passed and they were tired. "Let's go outside and get some fresh air," Ted said. "I agree," John said. Let's go." At that moment, Mrs. Baggins came in with two cups of coffee and cookies and said, "Where are you going?" "I just brought coffee".

"We'd better eat these in the yard," Ted said. And then he took the cups of coffee and cookies from his mother and they went to the yard with John. John stared at the house across the street where he had grown up, reviewing his memories. The house was different from that time; since no one had gotten there, all the flowers had dried up the house was dirty, and the yard was full of leaves that had fallen to the ground in the fall. One of the windows in the room was broken; it was as if someone wanted to enter the house. "How long has this house been empty?" John asked Ted.

Ted replied, "It has been almost a year since anyone has lived here. I do not know why the owner of this house no longer rents this place! "They say the owner is not here".

"I loved her so much," John said. "I had good days in this house." And it occurred to him to take a picture of the building. So without saying a word, he went and brought the camera...

"Where did you go without saying anything?" Ted said.

"I wanted to take a picture of this building as a souvenir," John said. A feeling tells me, how many more times this building will collapse. I wanted to take a picture of it before this happened; Just wish! It could have been the same as before to get the right picture.

"What do you think?" Said Ted. "Now, what is a building that you want to photograph"?

Without taking Ted's answer, John took a picture of the building. He lowered the camera to see the photo he had taken, and again another strange occurrence ... The picture he took was similar to the old house. "Ted ... Ted, I understand how this camera works," John shouted happily.

"What do you say, John?" Ted said. "Does that mean it's like that camera with extraordinary power"?

"Yeah, right," John said. With this camera, you can take the old shape of the place you want. I had tried this before in my room, but at that time I did not know what to ask for the camera, or maybe there did not change at all, but now in my mind I all wanted my picture to be the same as the old house; "In the same old way, the camera did the same thing for me".

"I'm happy, but it probably won't work for me either," Ted said. So it is useless; "So now give me the picture and let me see how it goes." John handed the camera to Ted and Ted looked at the picture and said, "Very interesting! Exactly as it was; "Like when you were here." Then he took another picture, and after seeing the picture, he said, "I said it would not work for me ... Come and get this." When John tried to take the camera, he pressed a button and suddenly a piece of printed paper came out of the camera, and the last-minute picture that Ted took came out.

"Did you see Ted?" John said. "With this camera, we can also print the photo we took." And then he saw the photo. The date of that day was on the photo. John also printed the other photo and saw the date on the photo; the date was the same year that John lived there. John was overjoyed to finally understand how to work with the camera, and said to Ted, "Although we could not find anything special about the island today, as soon as we realized the performance of this camera, it was very good." Ted was very happy to have that camera, too, but not as much as John.

"This camera works a lot in travel," Ted said. John nodded in agreement, and they both happily went inside. It was getting a little dark, and Mrs. Baggins was cooking. When she saw that they were happy, he smiled at Ted and said, "I have not seen you so happy for so long"!

"Yeah, Mom," Ted said, "something happy happened to me and John today".

"I hope good things always happen to you," Ms. Baggins said.

Ted and John headed for the room, and Mrs. Baggins said, "The food will be ready in an hour, and so your father will come".

"Okay, Mom," Ted said. "Whenever my father comes, tell us to come." And they entered the room and started searching and talking about that camera and the island and what they had to do...

An hour passed and Ted's father came; Mrs. Baggins called them downstairs for dinner. After washing their hands, Ted and John went to the kitchen and greeted Mr. Baggins. Mr.

Baggins had treated Ted better, and Ted was no longer doing the old-fashioned thing, and he was polite to people. Mr. Baggins, realizing that his son had behaved better since John returned, had treated him better; also, his treatment of John was very good. Ted also noticed the change in his father's behavior and was happy that John was back.

Everyone was sitting around the table eating; "Tonight dinner is as good as ever," John said, and Mrs. Baggins thanked him. After a few minutes, Mr. Baggins began to speak, saying, "A man came to the garage today to repair his car. I did not like him much. His eyes were evil. He was talking about the house in front of us. " He asked where the owner of the house was and whether anyone lived there now."

"What did you tell him, father?" Ted said fearfully.

"What did you mean, son?" Said Mr. Baggins. "I said it was being evacuated and no one knew where the owner was".

" What were the characteristics of this man, father?" Said Ted.

"A man of medium height, with brown hair and stubble," Mr. Baggins said. "Why are you asking this question"?

"Nothing father," Ted said. There is an evil man whose definition I heard. I said maybe he is the same person and he will come and be our neighbor; His characteristics were almost the same".

"Oh, what a pity," said Mr. Baggins. "If he is, it will be very bad for us".

"Yeah, Dad, it's not good at all," Ted said. We must also be careful; "Because the house is empty, no one should go there and stay there without news".

John just listened as Ted and his father talked. Fear had taken over his whole being. John guesses that the man must be Dallahan; That is, he was always watching over John and following him. It was scary for John to even think about it. He had previously felt that Dallahan was chasing him, but he had never felt so close. Ted, who was sitting next to John, noticed this change in John's behavior and state, and realized what he was thinking about; therefore, he hit John's foot very gently from under the table. John came to his senses and looked at Ted, and Ted noticed him by pointing to pull himself together and eat his food, and he began to eat to get a little away from it. After the meal was over and he talked for a while, it was time for John to go to the restaurant, and Mr. Baggins and Ted took John to the restaurant. "Take care of yourself," Ted said as he said goodbye. "If you see anything suspicious, be sure to let me know".

"Okay, Ted," John said, "take care of yourself too and keep an eye on the building".

After saying goodbye to Ted and his father, John went to his room to sleep, but could not sleep. He thought all night about the Dallahan; because he is very close to them and when they want to go to Bora Bora Island, they have to move in a way so that no one notices that they are leaving. John finally went to sleep, but once again he had the same dream he had had before. When he woke up in the morning, he was scared. John wondered what this dream could mean and what message it conveyed to John that he had seen the scene again. John got out of bed and got ready for work that day. That day, all the time, his mind was on Dallahan and his nightmare. He wanted to know the connection between his dream and Dallahan. At lunchtime, Mr. Gerard inquired about John when he saw him in that condition. After a short pause, John said that he was fine.

It was afternoon; John remembered the camera and that half-photo inside the black object. He decided to take another photo of that half photo with the camera to see the full face of the photo. After work, he went to his room and took a camera and a photo; in his mind, he reviewed the time before the photo has been cut and took the photo and printed it. When he saw the printed photo, the same man that John had dreamed of was in the other half. John was very surprised why the man's photo was cut! Why did they do that? John looked at the date of that photo; the photo was almost from ten years ago!

Every day, the secrets and mysteries of John's life were added and John tried to solve them so that the riddle of his life would end so that he could have a comfortable life.

The next day, John asked Ted to come there, and John shared the matter with Ted and showed him the photo. "He does not know this man and has never seen such a man before," Ted said as he saw the photo.

It had been almost a week since the island mattered and they had no way to get to that part of the sea. Due to Ted and John's age, they could not go to sea by diving; they were not even allowed to go to sea.

One day Mr. Havins came to the kitchen at rest time and looked for John. When he saw John, he said to John with a surprised face, "It does not seem to you to talk to such people"!

"Is something wrong, Mr. Havins? John asked. "What are you talking about"?

"I did not think you were in contact with these people," Mr. Havins said. "So close that he calls you John and remembers you well".

"What happened, Mr. Havins?" John said. "I'm dying of worry... please tell me what happened"?

"An old man with a smiling face came up to you," Mr. Havins said. I asked him what a man like him has to do with you. And that gentleman answered that he saw you in the library. He says you are a very good boy and praised you. Do you go to the library? Well done my son! Very good".

"Yes, Mr. Havins," John said, "where is he now"?

"I told him to sit in a chair, in the room, so you could go there, my son," Mr. Havins said.

John was surprised that Mr. Havins behavior had changed. Mr. Havins now had a special respect for John, now that he saw that a distinguished person, such as Professor Baxter, has word with John and admiring him. "Hurry up, son," Mr. Havins continued. Go, he is waiting for you. It is not good to procrastinate this man too much. "If you need anything, tell me to bring it to you".

John thanked Mr. Havins and went upstairs. With the information given by Mr. Havins, he was sure that Professor Baxter had come there, but he did not know why he had come. His mind was on this until he reached out to Mr. Baxter. John reached the top of the stairs and entered the hall. Seeing John, Professor Baxter said, "Oh ... my son! How're you? So you work here? Good place. I remember coming here and eating; Let me see how your cook is. So what's up? what have you done"?

"I'm fine, Professor," John said. "With what"?

"With that letter," said Professor Baxter.

" Professor, no one here knows that I read such a book," John said as he saw that Mr. Havins approached them. "Please do not say anything in front of Mr. Havins and we will talk about it later if possible".

Mr. Havins arrived with two cups of coffee and placed them on the table, saying, "Excuse me, sir!" "I feel like I saw you somewhere, but I do not remember everything I thought".

"Maybe you've seen me on TV or in the newspaper," said Professor Baxter, smiling.

"Yeah, right ... Right," Mr. Havins said. I saw you on TV. "You were talking about old manuscripts and how old manuscripts are and how many types of manuscripts there are in the world"...

"Yes, that's right," said Professor Baxter. I talked about that. "Do you like things like that"?

"Yes, Professor Baxter ..." Mr. Havins said, "I remember your name now." Yes, I'm generally interested in history and archeology and everything related to antiquity, and I always follow such programs. "I am very happy to see that one of the staff here is in contact with someone like you".

John was both happy and sad to learn that Professor Baxter was a well-known figure. He was glad that he had a friendship with such a person, and he was upset that he had seen the professor, but did not know him; because he was not watching TV. "I'm going to leave you alone," Mr. Havins said after a moment's talk. Professor Baxter thanked and Mr. Havins left. After Mr. Havins left, Professor Baxter said to John, "My son, I know that the text you have translated is part of a letter that belongs to you, and I know that you want to follow it. I did very thorough research on the place described in that letter and found that the island of Borabora is in France. You probably came to that conclusion yourself, but the important thing you probably know is that going to that point on the sea and going underwater is hard work and requires skilled labor; You are alone and you cannot do this, but my daughter works on that island and luckily for us her job is diving; He works in a research team that is on the island. I came here to say that I can help you with what you want to achieve; Of course, all I want is for you to give me an old copy of the book or something I can do; just that. my son! If I had wanted to, I could have gone to that treasure without telling you, but I did not. Because I'm not looking for money and I do not have such morals. My daughter lives there; you can trust me. I do not want you to answer now; "You can think and answer later".

Mr. Baxter got up and went to the front door, saying, "Goodbye, son." "Take care of yourself and think well of what I have to say." And then went out the door.

John was sitting there in a chair, thinking of Professor Baxter's words. To what he should do. That taking Professor Baxter is both good and bad; Well, in the sense that he has all the facilities that John wants, and he gave him the help that John was looking for, but in the sense that someone else is added to them, and it is possible that when they find the treasure, something goes wrong, it was not good. John was in these thoughts that Mr.Havins brought him to himself. Mr. Havins had come to talk to Professor Baxter. When he did not see Mr. Baxter, he asked John, "Did Mr. Baxter leave?" "Yes, Mr. Havins," John replied.

"How soon is he going?" Said Mr. Havins. I just wanted to talk to him. It was a pity. "Is he coming here again"?

"Maybe," John said. I do not know. "Maybe he will come again".

"Well done, my son," said Mr. Havins. It is good to associate with such people. He is a great man. You can learn new things. "Yes, very good." And then he picked up the cup of coffee and left. John went to the kitchen after Mr. Havins left to continue his work. John decided to tell Ted tomorrow; so he asked Ted to come there tomorrow afternoon at rest time.

Ted came to the restaurant the next day, and John told the story of Professor coming to the restaurant and his offer. Ted thought for a moment, and after a few minutes said, "I think he'd better come with us; because he seemed to be right, and according to him, if he wanted to, he could go there alone; Without you noticing. This means honesty and knowledge and on the other hand, his daughter is there and she can solve all the problems we have. I think this is a good thing and it is God's will that this man is on our way; it's true"?

"Yeah Ted, I'm thinking the same thing, and I think it's better if he comes," said John, thinking of Ted's talk. So today I call him and say that I accept his offer. "It's just a matter of time before we have to talk to the professor in person." And he said to Ted, "Wait a moment here for me to get the professor's number to call him." And then he went to the restaurant, and a few minutes later he went back to the kiosk in front of the restaurant and got the professor's number. A man picked up the phone and said, "Professor Baxter's office; Please ...

"I'm sorry," John said. I'm John Wilson. "Is the professor there?"

"Yes, but he is doing something," the man said. "Please give me your number so he can contact you".

"I wanted to talk to him," John said. "If you tell him I called, he would come on the phone".

The man said, "Very well; "Hold the phone for a moment to tell him".

A few moments later, Professor Baxter's voice was heard over the phone: "Hello, John. Did you decide my son? "I hope the answer is yes".

"Hello, Professor," John said. Yes, I decided. "Ted and I talked and you better come too".

"You did a wise job," the professor said. Be sure that I can be a good help to you. Well, now when do you decide to go?

"I wanted to see you tomorrow, if possible, to talk about when to go and what we need," John said.

"Very well," said the professor. "If you can, come to my office tomorrow at five o'clock to talk".

"Okay, Professor," John said. So I see you. Goodbye." The professor said goodbye and hung up the phone.

John turned to Ted and said, "We must go to the professor's office tomorrow; "Be here at four o'clock in the afternoon to go together".

"Do you have his address?" Ted said.

"Yes, I have the professor's business card," John said.

John was separated from Ted. When he entered the restaurant, he went straight to Mr. Truffaut's office to take leave for tomorrow, but Mr. Truffaut was not there. As he walked into the kitchen, he saw Mr. Havins and asked, "You do not know where Mr. Truffaut is"?

Mr. Havins replied, "He was busy and left early; He will not be here tomorrow either. Do you have a word"?

"I wanted to take a leave of absence from Mr. Truffaut for tomorrow afternoon," John said. What should I do now"?

"You can go tomorrow," Mr. Havins said. Of course, if Mr. Gerard has no problem; "I will tell Mr. Truffaut myself".

The next afternoon, Ted arrived at the time and they went to the professor's office together. The professor's office was in a tall tower on the 58th floor of the 1125 unit. When John entered, the building guard asked who they were dealing with, and John introduced himself and said that he has word with Professor Baxter. The guard said he had already coordinated and gave Ted and John the address of the professor's unit. Ted and John went to the elevator reached the professor's office and knocked on the door. The door opened and they entered and sat in the waiting room. A few minutes later, Professor Baxter entered the hall from another room and said, "Hello boys."Did you have a problem coming here"?

"No, Professor, we came easily," John said. And Ted greeted the professor. The professor led them to his room, and they both sat down on chairs. "Very well," said the professor. "When do you decide to go"?

"I can work in the restaurant for another week until the end of this month," John said. "Then we can go".

"Very well," said the professor. I think it's a good time to travel. We will coordinate our programs this week. I will call my daughter tomorrow and say that we want to go there. I tell my office manager to book three tickets for another week tomorrow as soon as possible so we can get to work as soon as possible. "I will tell you the flight time".

"What items should we bring with us?" John said.

"You do not need to bring much," the professor said. "only essential and personal accessories".

"Very well," John said. "So we are waiting for your news".

Ted was silent all this time, just listening, and then he said goodbye to the professor, and they left. They walked to Ted's house. "Tomorrow I will talk to Mr. Truffaut and tell him that I will not be able to work here for another week," John said on the way.

Ted and John arrived home. After dinner, John asked Ted if he knew about the building across the street.

"Yeah," Ted said, "a few days ago, I went inside the building and looked around. No one seemed to be coming; we do not think the person we think came there; "Of course, I hope so".

John returned to the restaurant and slept peacefully in his room. In a dream, he saw his childhood playing in the yard of that building.

A few days after John and Ted's last meeting with Professor Baxter, the professor called John and said that their flight ticket was for another week. John had told Mr. Truffaut that he was no longer working there. The kitchen staff was all upset that John was gone. Mr. Gerard and Mr. Richard were more intimate with John. Saturday was John's last day of work. During that time, he had many hardships and joys with his colleagues. That night, John decided to go to Ted's house and they were scheduled to be together on Monday to arrange a trip. As he left, Richard, a little emotional, hugged John and said, "I miss you so much. Come here whenever you can; "I will be very happy to see you again." And the rest said goodbye to John. John came out with tears in his eyes and went to Ted's house.

They spend Sunday collecting essentials. Ted had told his mother he wanted to go somewhere for a fun trip with his friends. His father knew he was going with John and did not

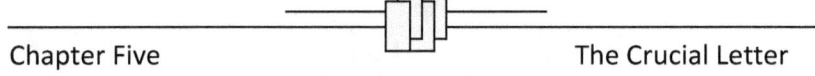
object. On Monday afternoon, they went to the professor's office to go to the airport.

Chapter Six

Travel to Bora Island

Professor Baxter is sitting in his office, waiting for John and Ted to arrive. Five hours left until the flight. After Ted and John arrived at the professor's office and had coffee, Professor Baxter's secretary picked them up at the airport and left New York at six o'clock in the afternoon for Paris. The professor said he had decided to stay in Paris for a day and had already booked a hotel; He also likes to show the sights of Paris to John as much as they have time.

While they were in Paris, the professor took them to the Eiffel Tower; at the foot of the Eiffel Tower, they took a souvenir photo. The next day they went to Pierrelate Airport in Tahiti and from there to Bora Bora. At Bora Bora Airport, Professor Baxter's daughter waited for them to arrive, and as soon as she saw her father, she hugged him tightly and said, " "Finally you came ... If you had nothing to do here, you would not have visited me, but now that you are here".

After greeting, the professor said to his daughter, "Ah ... I forgot to introduce you; Sorry guys!"Sarah, John, and Ted, and the boys, she is my daughter, Sarah".

John and Ted shook hands with Sarah, and Sarah greeted them and guided them to the car, and they all headed for Sarah's house.

Sarah's house was near the beach; it was a small town for the research team and Sarah lived there. When they entered the area, several people were there to greet them, and Sarah introduced her father to them. "I leave you alone to rest," Sarah said as she entered the house and showed the room to rest. "I will see you in the afternoon." So they had the opportunity to rest for a few hours.

In the afternoon and after a break, Sarah called her father for coffee. The professor also called John and Ted. They were all sitting in the hall drinking coffee when Sarah started talking and said, "Very well; Father, when should we start our work? I got permission from the company for a few days so that we could do our job. We must conclude as soon as possible; "Because I do not have much time".

"John is the decision-maker," the professor said. And he smiled at John and continued, "Isn't that so, John?" "You are the leader of the group and you have to say when we should go for what you want".

"Please, Professor," John said. I think if we start tomorrow morning, it will be very good; "Because I do not think there is a chance to search today".

"That's right, John," Sarah said. It is better to take a short walk inside the island today and see different places here. do you agree"?

"I agree," John said. And he looked at Ted and the professor, and they agreed.

"Very well," Sarah said. We better get ready. I'm going to get the car ready; "You come too".

John got up and went to his room, picked up a bag containing special items and valuables, and went out with Ted. The professor had gone to the car before them and was sitting in a chair next to Sarah. Sarah took them around the island and showed them the beauties and took them to a beach restaurant that cooked French food for dinner. As soon as he ate the first bite, John said the name of the food and the ingredients used in it. "Have you been here before and eaten such food?" Sarah said in surprise. "because this food is only cooked here".

Ted replied instead of John, saying proudly, "No, he was not here; "But John lives in a French restaurant in the United States, assisted by a chef, who cooks authentic French food there".

"I'm very happy to talk to such people," Sarah said. "I was really happy".

John and Ted smiled contentedly, and John said, "We are glad to see you; "That someone like you can help us".

The day passed and the night arrived. John and Ted were in their room, thinking about what awaited them tomorrow. They hoped to reach a conclusion tomorrow and be able to return as soon as possible.

They woke up early the next morning. Sarah was preparing her diving gear; when she saw John and Ted, she said good morning to them and pointed to the breakfast table, and said that breakfast is ready. Professor Baxter had woken up before them and was drinking coffee. After saying good morning and having breakfast, they went to the beach with Sarah. Sarah had already prepared the boat; this required a well-equipped boat for exploration. It was as if that boat had been made for them; the boat had a captain's cabin and a room under the boat. They boarded a boat, and Sarah asked her father for the address of the place, and the professor showed the destination according to the contents of the letter and told them which part of the island to go to. They were about fifteen miles from the shore; So that the beach could no longer be seen. There are no ships or boats around; Sarah picked up her things and got ready to jump into the water. "You know what to look for, my daughter," said her father.

"Yes, Dad, look for a black rock," Sarah said. "I hope it can be found here." And then in front of us, she sat on the edge of the boat and jumped into the water from the back. It had been almost thirty minutes since Sarah had left, and she had not yet returned. During that time, none of the three people on the boat spoke. All three were thinking of finding that rock. Finally, Sarah grabbed the corner of the boat and got off it, and sat down in the corner of the boat. As soon as Sarah sat down, the three of them asked, "What happened?" "Did you find anything"?

Sarah smiled and said, "Let me pass a moment".

"I'm sorry," John said. "We were in a hurry".

"I went here for a mile, and I went to a depth of two thousand feet, but I did not find anything," said Sarah. "I'd better go a little further and look there".

After a short break, Sarah took the boat a few miles. The boat stopped, and Sarah got ready to fall into the water again. When Sarah left, Ted said very quietly, "You'd better use your tools." John did not understand Ted and said, "What should I use"?

"With that Binoculars, you can see the rock," Ted said.

"Yeah, right," John said. "It can be done".

"Just act in a way that the professor does not understand what you are doing," Ted said.

"Yeah, I got it," John said. I am careful." Then he took the Binoculars out of his bag, and in his mind, he associated the location of the rock with the full address in the letter and placed the camera in front of his eyes. He saw the black rock through the camera lens; so there was that rock. "That's what we're looking for should be here," he told Ted. "I'm seeing it".

"Look around that rock, can you find any clues?" Ted said.

John looked carefully and saw that a small boat had fallen near the rock and sank. There was an inscription in French on the boat, but John could not read it completely due to the erosion of the boat. John looked around the rock again and saw a large seven-colored stone at a distance from the rock. That, too, could be a good sign; John was telling Ted the pictures he saw.

"Would you like to see Sarah around to find out if there is a black rock at all?" Ted said.

John looked around them in his mind and asked the Binoculars to show them underwater. Down below he saw Sarah searching underwater. It was about two miles away. John did not see the signs he had seen around the rock, where Sarah was. "I do not think this is the place of the Black Rock," he told Ted.

"I wish we could know our distance from there and know which way to go," Ted said.

"Yeah, if that happened then it would be great," John said.

John picked up his camera again and looked at the black rock. He wanted to see if he could find a sign that was relevant here. As he held the Binoculars, he rotated it around and wanted to see the image up close, so he inadvertently decided to rotate the camera lens. John saw the geographical coordinates of the place in the image from the camera. "I learned another function of the Binoculars" John happily told Ted.

"What function?" Said Ted.

"By rotating this lens, it shows you the coordinates of the place you are looking at," John said.

"That's great," Ted said. "It is better to see the geographical coordinates of this point and take notes".

John did the same, writing down both coordinates and saying, "Now we know where to go; "We just have to wait for Sarah to come".

"There's a boat that something is written on it," John said. I want to read it; but it does not happen; "Because part of it has been erased".

"It doesn't matter," Ted said. "You can take a picture of the boat's past with that camera and read the text before it is erased".

John said, "Well done, Ted!" You are so smart; "But we cannot go underwater and take pictures of it".

"If we could go underwater ourselves, a lot of our problems would be solved," Ted said.

Professor Baxter has been studying in the downstairs room since Sarah went into the water. "When he came up, John and Ted were talking about the coordinates of the place and discussing how to tell the professor not to doubt".

The professor reached out to the two and said, "What's up guys?" You are talking hard. "Well, let me know what you were talking about".

Ted and John said to each other, "About ..." John looked at Ted and continued, "About these numbers that I had already taken from the original letter in my hand. I do not know what these numbers mean! We were talking about this. Ted was saying that maybe these are codes, but I'm saying that with these symbols above these numbers, I do not think they are codes. These must be things we do not know. "Professor, you know what these are".

"Let me see what," said the professor.

John handed the sheet to the professor, noting the coordinates of the first point of the same place on the Black Rock. When the professor saw it, he said, "These are the geographical coordinates of a place."Wait and see ... maybe this address is the same as the Black Rock".

"If that's true, that's great," John said. "There is no need to look elsewhere anymore".

"Yeah, right," Ted said. "Our time will not be wasted".

The professor said, "Yes, that's right, but we have to wait until Sarah arrives to find the place we want from these numbers; "Because I do not know either".

The three men, happy to find out, went into the cabin and poured themselves three cups of coffee and drank coffee to get Sarah out of the water. A few minutes later, Sarah came out of the water. As soon as they heard Sarah come out of the water, the three of them went to her and helped her. Sarah, who looked tired, got on the boat, sat down on a chair, and after a short rest, drank a cup of coffee. "My daughter, we found a geographical coordinate that I think is the characteristics of the place we have to go," the professor said. You should see this and comment; "Where are these coordinates"?

Sarah took the paper from her father and looked at it carefully. Now, we do not have time to go there; Because we are slowly approaching the darkness of the air. By the way, I am very tired and I cannot dive again. "We'd better leave it for tomorrow".

"Okay, my daughter," said the professor. Tomorrow is better; "Because we are going there with more energy".

After a while, Sarah took them to the shore. After the boat was moored, they went to the dock and got in the car, and went home to rest. After dinner, John and Ted went to their room to talk more freely about the day's events, as well as the boat which was underwater and so on. Ted had different opinions. They were more afraid that someone would find the treasure they were looking for and that they would not find anything else; because, as it turned out, it was as if someone had already gone to that treasure. After various comments and conversations, they fell asleep on their bed.

When John fell into a deep sleep, he dreamed that he was swimming underwater, next to the boat. Inside the boat was a human skeleton with a large ring with a black jewel on its left finger; It was as if the man had been chained to a boat; because the metal was around the skeleton's hand. In the dream world, John could not get himself into that boat no matter how hard he tried. It was as if the more he swam towards the boat, the more the opposite current intensified and did not allow him to reach that boat. John woke up; It was morning and they had to get out of bed to get ready to go to that particular place. John washed his hand and face and woke Ted. Ted hardly got up. When they went downstairs, the professor and Sarah were awake, setting the breakfast table, and saying good morning to Ted and John. After breakfast, they went to the pier and boarded a boat to get to their destination. John and Ted were stressed to go there; "Can they find that treasure?" An hour later, they reached the point where they had found the coordinates. Sarah got ready to dive. "I hope we can find that rock here," Sarah said. And then she went to the edge of the boat and fell into the water. "It's better to see what Sarah is doing with the

Binoculars," Ted said after Sarah left. John accepted Ted's offer, picked up the camera, and looked at the location of the black rock with the camera. Sarah was nearby, approaching the rock.

When Sarah saw the rock, she spun around to find a hole or crevice where the treasure may have been hidden but found nothing. After spinning, Sarah caught sight of the boat; As John had dreamed, a skeleton inside the boat caught Sarah's attention and she swam towards it, but the harder she tried, the less she got closer. It was as if a force was blocking Sarah from reaching the boat. Sarah tried several times to reach that boat; but it was useless, she could not get herself there. When she saw that it was useless, she got tired of it and decided to come to the top of the water and rest a little and try again; so she went back to the surface of the water and got herself into the boat. John, Ted, and the professor were waiting for Sarah, and as soon as they saw Sarah, they lifted her, and after a short rest, she told the story of the underwater and told it about the boat. And that she could not get herself into the boat. John and Ted felt frustrated and thought that they had reached the end of the line and that there was nothing there, and that they wasted their time in vain. Seeing their faces, Professor Baxter smiled and said, "Boys, why are you disappointed? This is just the beginning. The first time you cannot find what you want; now, by finding the coordinates of this point, our work is ahead more. We have to look more closely and first of all, find the reason for not getting to that boat, why can't we go to it? "There must be a specific reason".

Hearing the professor's words, John felt hopeful and said, "Yes, that's right, professor. There must be a specific reason; "What do you think, Ms. Baxter"?

Sarah smiled and said, "It's better to call me Sarah, John. I also think my father is right. We need to look there more closely and also study the location of that boat more closely; Maybe from a geological point of view, there is a phenomenon that we are unaware of. I did not come across such a case during the whole time I was researching this island. "I must talk to my friends about this".

"Better not to do that," the professor jumped in between Sarah. You make them curious about this point and they rush here and make our job harder. "You'd better talk to your friends after we're done".

"Yes, father, you are right," Sarah said.

"Now what do you say we do?" Said Ted, who had been listening to them all this time.

"We'll be here again tomorrow, and Sarah will look at the rock again, maybe she'll find a hole," said the professor. "So we'd better go home now and rest a little".

"Today, I'm cooking so Sarah can taste my cooking," said John, who wanted to change the atmosphere.

"How good," said the professor. Well, for Sarah's sake, we can eat your handicrafts; "Otherwise, you would not have given us food now"...

Embarrassed, John lowered his head and the professor said he was joking. They all went home, and that night John followed one of the book's recipes and made delicious food. The professor and Sarah, as well as Ted, were amazed at the taste of the food after it was eaten and that a boy of John's age could make it. "This is amazing," Sarah said. "I have never tasted such a taste in my whole life".

"He is my friend ..." said Ted, "in the kitchen, after the chef, he was cooking food".

John turned a little red and embarrassed. "Enough," said the professor. "Otherwise, there will be nothing left of John and he will melt." And everyone laughed together. John was so happy that night that he was able to show his skill to his friends once again. He had a good night's sleep that night.

The next morning, they headed for the Black Rock again. After Sarah got ready, she fell into the water and John looked at Sarah again with the camera and reported to Ted what was happening. After much searching, Sarah again came up with no results and went back to the top of the water and explained. John thought he had to go there himself. Probably only John can see there; Like the camera that only John could use. It was in these thoughts that John said aloud, "I want to see myself there".

Everyone was surprised by John's words; Because Sarah was defining underwater issues, but because John was drowning in his thoughts, he could not hear Sarah talking. When he saw that everyone was looking at him in amazement, he realized what had happened and said, "Excuse me! "I was thinking and I was not aware at all".

"What were you thinking?" Ted said.

"I should see it up close," John said. "Maybe I can relate to the text I read".

"It's not so easy to go underwater," Sarah said. For that depth! "You have to be trained".

"Well, if you can, teach me," John said.

Sarah said, "Oh, you cannot in this short time; we do not have much time. Also, my vacation time is coming to an end; "We do not have the opportunity to do that".

Professor Baxter jumped in between his daughter and said, "Do you not know anyone else who can teach?" John who does not want to dive professionally comes down with you and comes back with you. It is enough to learn as much. John just wants to see it up close. "Maybe it will solve the problem of this puzzle." John was happy that the professor had supported him, so he looked at the professor and then said, "Please, Sarah! This is very important to me. I spent a lot of time on this. I do not want to go through it so easily. There must be a connection there; "I feel like I can find something." "Very well," Sarah said after John's insistence. I cannot, but I introduce you to my friend to teach. He is a professional diver. "I think he can teach you what to do in the little time we have, as much as we want".

After the diving training discussion was over, they returned home, and Sarah spoke to her friend on the phone, and it was decided that they would visit Sarah's friend together in the morning to begin their training. That night, after Ted and John went to the room to rest and were alone together, Ted said to John, "What are you thinking, John"?

"I think when I get there, the flow that won't let Sarah into the boat will probably stop," John said. Maybe it just stops when I go; "As I was the only one who could work with the Binoculars".

"I hope so," Ted said. Anyway, until you get there, you cannot understand; But I concluded that I should come with you. I will be training from tomorrow. "It's not good to send you there alone".

"I'm not alone," John said. "Sarah is with me".

"Okay, but I'll come with you," Ted said. I do not want to hear anything anymore. "Tell Sarah that Ted will come tomorrow".

"Okay, Ted," John said. "if you want to come with me, no problem".

Early in the morning, after breakfast, John told Sarah that Ted also wanted to learn to dive; Because Ted wants to accompany me too. After a bit of grumbling, Sarah accepted, and then they went to a place where Sarah's friend, Abraham, was. The professor was at home; because he did not need to come with them. Sarah introduced John and Ted to Abraham and explained how much they wanted to learn diving and those they did not have much time to do so, and then went to work with her. After Sarah left, Abraham began training and explained the basics to them. John and Ted returned home after completing their training. When they arrived; the professor was studying and seeing them, he said, "A gentleman came here today".

"Who was he?" John and Ted said.

"He did not introduce himself correctly," the professor said. But he had a face that I will not forget and the eyes that one was afraid to look at; he had stubble. He asked a series of unanswered questions and left. I think he was suspicious. It was as if he was looking for something else; "I felt this way from the incomprehensible questions".

Hearing those words from the professor, Ted and John were terrified. How could Dallahan get there! The professor did not see their faces at that moment; otherwise, he would have doubted them. John and Ted went to their room. They could not do anything at the moment; John had previously told Ted that the closer they got to the treasure, the more they would see Dallahan; It is as if Dallahan is deliberately showing himself to them to say that I am close to you.

It took a week for John and Ted to train enough to dive once with Sarah. Although Abraham still disagreed and did not consider the training sufficient, and his view was that they should be trained for at least a month, John and Ted could no longer tolerate it. Abraham also took responsibility for this on them and forbade them from doing so; So Ted and John decided to continue training for another week. After the two-week training was over, Sarah took another time, and the next day they went to the Black Rock site again. This time, Sarah also brought a means of communication to communicate with her father underwater. Because it was Ted and John's first real dive, they were a little stressed.

"Do not be afraid," Sarah said. I am with you. There is no problem; "Just do not stay away from me".

They went underwater and Sarah led them both to the Black Rock. John himself saw it up close and looked at the rock carefully, and it seemed that there was a hole in the rock. He put his hand on the part and then asked Sarah to go to the boat and all three went to the boat, but John's move to the boat was useless. Like Sarah, she failed to do so; John returned and asked Sarah to return to the surface of the water. When they reached the top of the water, the professor was waiting for them. John raised his head and sat down on a chair without speaking. Ted sat down next to him and said nothing. "What happened?" The professor said a few minutes later. "Did you see anything there"?

"I have to think about it," John said. Maybe I can find a connection. John got up and went downstairs. Ted followed him. John went to his bag and took out the black stone and took it in his hand. Surprised by John's behavior, Ted said after giving John a chance to think, "Well ... what did you conclude?" "What are you thinking about at all"?

Overwhelmed, John raised his head and said, "Did you say something"?

"I mean, what do you think?" Ted said. "Did you think so deeply that you did not notice my presence"?

"I think this rock is a piece of that rock," John said. When I looked closely at that rock, I noticed a depression on the rock that did not look natural; It is as if a part of the rock has been separated. The depression was similar to this rock. I feel that this stone has a force and something must be done. So far, everything I took from that dumpster has worked for me except this stone. I was always thinking about what this stone is for, but now I know what it is for; "We have to go back underwater so we can try this".

"Okay," Ted said. so why the delay? "Move on."

When they got on the boat, Sarah and the professor were talking, and when they saw Ted and John, they stopped talking. "What happened my son?" The professor said to John. "Did you conclude?

"Let's go down again to see what happens," John said.

The professor noticed something in John's hand and said, "What is that in your hand"?

"Nothing," said John, wrapping the black object in a cloth so that the professor would not doubt its black color. "I need it for underwater." "We can go underwater again," he told Sarah.

"Okay," Sarah said. "We still have time to go down one more time".

All three were ready to go underwater. When they reached that place, John went straight to the Black Rock and looked for the same depression. When he found the depression, he inserted a black object. And he looked at the rock surrounding him to find something new but saw nothing special. Suddenly Ted turned to John and noticed him on the boat. It was as if no current was coming out of it. Seeing this scene, John swam towards the boat and reached the boat very easily. First of all, he went to the ring he had dreamed of. Without Sarah noticing, he picked up the ring and inspected the rest of the boat with Ted. Sarah reached out to them to help. Sarah was still puzzled by how that water escape had been cut off. John told Sarah a key, as well as a locked door, that we should go upstairs. Sarah swam up, but John went to the object and picked up the stone first. And the flow started again.

The three of them set off to get to the surface of the water and reached the boat, where they fell from exhaustion to catch their breath. After their excitement subsided, John went to the box. The others were looking at John as something was happening. He dropped the key in his hand and locked it. The lock was unlocked and John anxiously opened the box door. There were a lot of coins inside the box and a piece of paper on the box door. John picked up the paper and placed it next to the same black stone. After finishing seeing the coins, he just noticed that others were looking at him; everyone was surprised. "Why do you look at me like that?" John said with a smile.

"You finally found it," said the professor.

"Yeah, I think so," John said.

"Good boy," Ted said. "Well done".

"The lightning strikes your eyes," Sarah said.

"It's better to put these in another container," John said. "Because if we take like this, it will attract attention and we will decide about it at home".

"I'm going to go down the cabin," Sarah said. "I think we have something to put these in." and hurried down to the cabin. The professor went to the box and said, "May I see one of these"?

"Please, Professor," said John. and handed one of the coins to the professor.

The professor examined the coin carefully to see if he could guess its history to find the coinage period.

Sarah turned from the bottom and brought another box that was bigger than the coin box. He gave it to John and put it in a larger box, closed the door, and said, "We'd better get out of here now".

Sarah went to the helm and started the engine and headed for the beach. All this time, Ted had not spoken to John. After seeing the professor busy with the coin and Sarah steering the boat, he went ahead and said very quietly, "What do you want to do now"?

"What do you mean?" Said, John.

Ted said, "You'd so dumb, don't be so silly!"I mean coins".

"Oh ... Well, we'll share," John said.

"Why divide it?" Ted said. This was your share; "Family inheritance ... you saw that the dumpster just gave you the address.

"I think these coins are so many that if they are divided into four, they will reach everyone so that we can live very comfortably for the rest of our lives," John said.

"But oh ..." Ted said.

"Don't think about it too much," John said. Let's get home. It is better to be divided; It has less trouble. Ted lowered his head and thought about it and sat down on a chair. Each of them was thinking. Sarah smiled contentedly on her lips and it was clear that she was dreaming. Ted, with a suspicious face, subdued the others with suspicion. The professor was still flipping the coin up and down, looking back and forth to get something out of it, and John was thinking about that boat and the black rock. When they reached the beach, so that no one would suspect, they put the trunk in the car and headed home. Sarah was afraid someone would chase them.

"My daughter, no one knows what we have who wants to chase us," the professor said.

They entered the house and placed the box in the middle of the room, between the sofas, and all four of them sat on the sofa. A few minutes passed in silence. Then the professor said: "My son, it is better to sell these and keep the money in your account; Because these coins are difficult to carry and will cause you trouble. One of my friends sells antiques; I can call him to sell these.

Sarah, who was upset with her father's word, had her eyebrows furrowed. She must have thought some of the coins is for herself and did not think his father would say so, but instead, Ted was happy for the professor to bring the matter up.

"No, Professor," said John, "I want these coins to be divided among the four of us, and everyone takes a share of it." The professor said, "No, my son, these coins were your right; I did not come to get these things." I do not need to, and my age no longer allows me to think about these things".

"It's not like that," John said. "So is Sarah".

The professor looked at Sarah and saw her upset face and said, "I do not think Sarah will need a share of these coins; "Is that right, my daughter"?

"Oh ... yes, Dad," Sarah said sadly.

"I do not like to ignore your troubles," John said. And he started counting and asked Ted to help him. When the counting of coins was over, John said, "It is fifty thousand coins." I want to tell you something; this is not a treasure; my family inheritance and the letter I gave you are part of another letter that my grandfather left me and I found its address. My father had come to this inheritance before, but unfortunately, he could not find it, and I finished it, but I would like to give this inheritance to you so that we can all share in this treasure. He gave Sarah 200 coins and said, "This is your share".

Sarah gladly accepted, but the professor did not accept the coins he gave him, saying, "I said I did not need them, and I will keep the same coin I took from you as a souvenir."I told you from day one why I wanted to go on this trip, but I did not get what I thought".

Ted also did not accept the coins and said, "I am your friend; "It was my duty to help and I did not do it for money".

 Sarah was embarrassed that she had accepted the coins and wanted to return them, but John said, "No need; You worked very hard and this is your right."I did it with full consent." Sarah was happy too and thanked John.

"I want to go there again," John continued. I think other things still could be found there. "That boat has many secrets".

"Yes, I do not think it will be over with this box," the professor said. "I would love to come too, but my age does not allow it".

"Can we go there again tomorrow?" John said to Sarah.

"Why not!" Said Sarah happily.

"I'd better call my friend so he can think of these coins," said the professor.

"It's better to hide these coins until the professor's friend arrives," John said.

"I have a secret place in the basement here that no one can find," Sarah said. "We'd better leave it there." And Sarah and John and Ted went there and hid the coins. When they returned, the phone was finished. the professor said that his friend would be here tomorrow night. John and Ted went to their room and Sarah went to her room. John was happy to get the coins and hoped they would get something tomorrow.

"I'm sure there are other things there," said John to Ted, "but I do not know why the boat sank and who's handcuffed."

John brought the ring and the paper and showed it to Ted and continued, "This ring was in his hand and this paper was in that box".

Ted pointed to the box and said, "in this box"?

"Did you bring this here?" John said.

"Yeah," Ted said. "I said we might find something else." "I brought it to search it on time".

John first opened the paper; the picture on the paper looked like a road map, but it was not clear where it was. He looked at the ring. On that ring was a piece of the same black object on which something was engraved. John was careful; the letters "j-w" were engraved. "I think the person in the boat is my grandfather," John said.

"How?" Said Ted.

John said, "Oh, this ring that was in his hand, the first letter of his name is engraved on it; "Like that black object whose name was engraved".

"It's getting so complicated," Ted said. I still have a question as to why your grandfather was handcuffed in that boat. I think he was killed and drowned, but why was that box there! "If someone wanted to kill him, why didn't he take the box"?

"Yeah," I said, "I thought about it, and I did not come to a conclusion like you." "I want to take another look at that boat," he said. Then he went to the Binoculars and examined the boat carefully. John became a little more careful and felt that something on the bottom of the boat was shining. He zoomed in on it, but the image was not clear. As he watched, he complimented Ted. He lowered the camera and said to Ted, "I'd better take the other things with me to the water tomorrow; I do not know! "But I think it will help me".

"But those things get wet," Ted said. "Maybe the camera will break down".

"I thought of that, too," John said. "I made a waterproof bag and put it in it".

"You are so clever, boy," Ted said.

"We'd better sleep," John said. "We have a lot of work to do tomorrow".

The next morning they went to the same place again and after getting ready for diving, they went underwater. When they reached that point, John, without hesitation, went to the Black Rock, but the object in its place, and cut off the flow. Then he went to the boat and picked the object up from the bottom of the boat. That object was a key. One of the skeleton hands was punched and something was closed in that fist. John pulled the object out of the bone of his hand. He put everything he could find in the bag; John had told Ted to explore the cliff with Sarah so he could explore the boat himself without interruption. Ted, who understood the situation, tried as much as he could to divert Sarah's attention. Among the items he found was a necklace around the neck of the skeleton. He picked it up and put it in the bag. And again he looked carefully all over the boat. He found a white object, resembling an orb, and when he saw nothing else in the boat, he went to Ted and Sarah and asked if they had found anything. Ted and Sarah had found items to show John. John signaled that they should return to the top, and they returned to the surface of the water and boarded the boat.

John had taken some old objects to show to the professor, but he did not show the main object. Sarah also has found a series of old pieces; Including a pistol and sword. Ted had found another skeleton nearby with his hand tied to a pole that had sunk into the rock. And the skeleton was sitting on the ground. Ted had not found anything special about that skeleton. The professor was even happier with the tools they had found this time and looked at them very carefully. "We'd better go back," John said. "I want to come here again tomorrow".

"But I do not think we can go back," Sarah said.

"If you allow me, we will come ourselves," John said. "Ted can work with this boat".

Sarah nodded a little and then said, "Okay." and returned home.

When they entered the house, they encountered a bad scene; everything was in disarray. It was clear that someone had come there and was looking for something special. John and Ted looked at each other and said, "Dallahan"!

"Who is Dallahan?" Said the professor.

John explained the Dallahan case to the professor; "Why didn't you tell me earlier?" said the professor. Isn't this the same man who came here that day? He was chasing us. "We need to inform the police sooner".

The professor called the police. John and Ted went to the coins after visiting all the rooms and making sure that no one was there, and after visiting, they were relieved that the coins were there.

"I said, 'This is a safe place,'" Sarah said.

The police arrived at the scene after twenty minutes and left after asking frequently asked questions. The professor gave them the Dallahan details. But John and Ted were worried that Dallahan would come to them. And when they got to their room, John showed Ted the key, the necklace, and the white orb. Ted also brought a sealed metal box, as well as a piece of metal that indicated it was part of an important box with old motifs on it.

"I found this in the skeleton hand," said Ted. It was as if he was holding this in his hand. "It must have been important".

"These are important," John said. "Tomorrow we will be much more comfortable when Sarah is not with us".

As the two were talking, they heard footsteps coming up the stairs. As soon as he heard the sound of footsteps, John put the items in a special bag. The sound of footsteps approached the door; it was Sarah. She knocked on the door and said, "Boys, my father's friend has come; "He wants to talk about coins".

Ted and John went downstairs without delay. The professor's friend was a tall man with a shaved head and influential eyes. Seeing John and Ted, he got up and shook hands with them, introduced himself, and said, "Hello. I'm Michael Rakhov; "I'm glad to meet you".

John and Ted shook hands, and John said, "Did you see the coins, Mr. Rakhov"?

"Yes, I saw the coins professor showed me," Rakhov said. "I want them all." And they traded and agreed on a price.

"It's better to give the account number to deposit the money into the account," professor said.

John gave the account number to Mr. Rakhov and the money transfer operation took place. When the coins were brought upstairs, Dallahan entered the room with another handgun. "Drop the coins so that no one gets hurt," Dallahan said. "I have been waiting for this moment for several years".

"I'm sorry," Mr. Rakhov said. Such a thing is not possible. "The coins are minnow, and I will not give them away at all".

Dallahan wanted to shoot Mr. Rakhov, but something hit his head hard and he fell to the ground. Dallahan's aide started firing, but Mr. Rakhov's bodyguards shot him and he was killed. Mr. Rakhov ordered his bodyguards to put the box in the car and told the professor, "The police shouldn't know about these coins."I will stay here to tell the story to the police".

Professor explained yesterday's case to Mr. Rakhov to keep up to date. They handcuffed the Dallahans so that the police could arrive. After the police arrived and interrogated Dallahan, as well as the others, they took Dallahan with them, and Mr. Rakhov went to the police station for further explanation. And they no longer saw Mr. Rakhov and did not understand what had happened to him. But John was happy that Dallahan was finally trapped and hoped to be punished. After the strange adventures that had happened to them, they felt very tired and all fell into a deep sleep.

The next day, when John woke up, his thoughts were on what had happened yesterday, as well as what he had seen underwater. He still wanted to go underwater. After Ted woke up, they went downstairs together and had breakfast with the professor and Sarah. Sarah had to go to work that day and could not take leave more than that. "Well, I think the work here is over and we have to go back," professor said. It is better to tour the island today and get our return ticket tonight. Well, it's as if I did not find what I was looking for. "Better yet, I'll not waste my time here".

"There's something I have to say," John said. I want to go underwater again. I think other things should be there. Now coins or anything; I do not think that's all that my ancestors left me. "One hundred percent must be something beyond what has been written with so much mystery".

"Yeah, I agree with John," Ted said.

"Oh, I cannot come," Sarah said.

"There is nothing wrong," John said. Only if you can give us the boat we will go. "I think we learned so much diving that we could go on our own".

"Did you see anything special there that you want to go back to?" Said professor. "Is there anything you did not tell us"?

"No, Professor," John said, "but I feel I have to look there again, more precisely".

"You can take that boat," Sarah said. "Just be very careful".

"Very well," said the professor. After breakfast, we go.

After breakfast, Sarah said goodbye to them and went to work, and John and Professor, and Ted went to the rock to explore further. On the way, John kept thinking about that black rock and other things. When they got there, John and Ted got dressed without delay and got ready to go underwater. "Be very careful," said the professor, who was found to be a little anxious. "If you see something special, let me know".

Ted and John dive into the water and moved straight toward the skeleton. John first put the black object in its place to cut off the flow of water, and then they both went to the boat to find something new. John was looking for something to convince the professor to stay there for a few more days; because if today he could not find anything for professor to investigate that would attract him, professor would leave and they would have to go back or tell the whole thing to the professor. John and Ted carefully searched all parts of the boat. John had decided to take another picture of the boat before it sank. When he looked more closely at the printed photo, he saw three people sitting in the boat; While John had found only one skeleton. It was as if the other two people had made this on the person who was in the water. John looked at the picture again. He felt he knew one of them. It looks like the same man he dreamed of, but this photo was from a few years ago and that person was living in the present, and surprised John. John has so engrossed in his thoughts that Ted came to John with an object in his hand. Ted had brought a piece of stone to John as if something had been written on it. John took the stone from Ted and was happy and said that this was what he wanted.

John motioned for Ted to return to the boat to rest. And they both went back to the boat. When professor saw them, he took a deep breath and said, "How are you"?

"Yes, Professor, we are very well," John said to the professor after he recovered a little. "We found something new that I think you will be happy to see".

Professor's eyes shone and said, "What?"Let me see my son".

John showed the object to the professor. Professor was delighted to see it and said, "Now this is the right thing to do. It turned out that I did not go all this way for no reason. "I think this is where my work will start".

"Professor. You have been working since you translated the text," John said, and then all three smiled in victory.

"We want to go back under the water after a little rest," Ted said. "Maybe we found something else there".

"Okay, go," said the professor, who was relieved this time. Yeah, I think a lot is going on there. "Look there well and accurately".

Professor, who was already drowning in the stone tablet, wanted to know what was written on the stone! The text of the stone was in the same script as the letter; it seems that John's ancestors were very interested in this script and knew that few people knew this.

John and Ted were sitting in the room talking about the necklace. John showed Ted a picture he had taken of the boat and talked about the resemblance of one of the people in the boat to the one he had dreamed of. "I hear weirder things about you every day," Ted said. It seems that these are not all and this is just the beginning. "What is your decision now"?

"With the tablet you found, we bought a few days until the professor is busy with that stone tablet. We can work on the tools we found to understand how they work and why," John said.

"Yeah, that's fine," Ted said. "We must first understand what these are so that we do not go underwater for any reason".

After a short rest, John and Ted went underwater to the same skeleton, but found nothing else, returned to the top without result, and then headed home. All three were very tired. By the time they got home, Sarah had arrived and prepared food for them. After eating, they told Sarah the story of the day and found the stone tablet, and showed it to Sarah. Sarah asked them if they were going to go to the water again tomorrow, and John replied that they would not go for a few days to see what was written on the tablet.

"That way I can come with you," Sarah said.

Professor was studying hard on that stone tablet and did not eat properly due to excitement. After talking to Sarah, John and Ted went to their room to rest and took out what they had found. Ted brought a rectangular piece of metal that was gold, but had no markings on it, and was flat. Ted and John put all the things they had found during this time together to see what they were worth. The strangest thing was the white rob. "Do you think this is like a witch ball that shows up in movies and can see anything you want?" Ted said.

"I do not think so," John said. If that's the case, it's not going to work; because with these Binoculars, I can see what I want. "I think it has other abilities".

John turned his attention to the box and the key and said, "Why haven't we tried this key on this box before"?

"I do not know," Ted said. "We were so involved in the issue of coins and Dallahan that we forgot what we found from the sea".

John picked up the box and turned the key in it; the box was unlocked. John opened the box door and looked inside. The inside of the box was full of strange motifs depicting creatures that John had never seen before. Inside the box, he found a larger, gold-colored key with a specially cut diamond, as well as a piece of leather with stripes on it, and a smooth, ornate piece of marble that something like a number was written on it, but it was not clear in what language.

"We should investigate what we found in the days that the professor has been researching the tablet," John said. For example, this thing that is engraved on stone or these lines that is on a piece of leather or those engravings. Ted picked up the gold-plated metal and the piece of metal he had removed from the skeleton and said, "Do you think the two pieces are related"?

"Anything is possible," John said. "They may be related".

John picked up the ring and necklace and said, "I think these two black pieces belong to that rock, and there must be another hole in that rock, and by putting these two pieces in their place, something else will happen; "Like when the water current was cut off".

"We have to go there and try," Ted said.

John examined the black object the dumpster had given him. After finding nothing, he stopped searching and placed it on a gold plate. Suddenly the black object began to spin, and light emitted from it illuminated the entire room. John and Ted stared at the light with their eyes wide with excitement and came to their senses when the light was off. John did not know where that light came from and what happened at all, but he did not feel good about it.

"It's better not to do it again," John said. "I do not think it will have good consequences".

"Yeah, I was scared of the light," Ted said. "I felt like it was swallowing us".

They were both silent for a moment. John picked up the other piece of metal and placed the stone on it, but this time nothing happened.

"What do you want to do?" Ted said.

"I want to see what other reactions we can see," John said.

It had been almost three hours since they had been in the room when Sarah's voice was heard calling them to eat. Ted and John put the items in the bag and went downstairs. Sarah was sitting in the kitchen waiting for them. John turned to the professor; "I called him out loud," Sarah said. He says he is coming now, but when his mind is busy, he does not think of anything else. "I am afraid he will faint from extreme hunger".

"I'm going to call him," John said. And then he went to the professor's room. He knocked but did not hear a sound. He opened the door and the professor was immersed in the study of ancient texts. John cleared his throat and said, "Professor, you better come for food." "It's time to move on".

The professor, who had just noticed John in the room, raised his head and said, "Oh ... John! you are here? I did not notice you at all; when did you come? what do you want"?

John reiterated that the food was ready and that they had better come to eat.

"Okay ... okay," said the professor. I'm coming".

"If you can, let's go now," John said. Because you told Sarah the same thing; "But you make yourself busy with reading it again".

At John's insistence, he dropped the book and went to the kitchen to eat. "I'm getting to good places," the professor said as he ate; "First I have to finish the book I am reading so that I can finish the translation work of that tablet".

"I'm sorry, Professor," said John, who saw the opportunity to ask questions. "Where can you see the numbers in this language"?

"In this book, I am reading, there are also numbers," the professor said. I can give you this book tomorrow; "did you find anything else".

"Yes," said John, "a piece of rock that something was written on it; "I think it's a number".

"I'd better see it," said the professor. "Maybe it's something else".

After eating, John showed the piece of stone to the professor. Professor took the piece of stone to his room, and John and Ted followed. In the book, professor was looking for a shape engraved on the stone. And in the book, he reached the number seven and said: "It is seven, but what it is related to, I do not know"!

John took the stone from the professor and thanked him and they went to their room. professor also start doing his job. John and Ted went to their room and slept. Again in the morning, they focused on the devices they had found so that they might find a clue or sign to solve the puzzle. "I want to go underwater one more time," John told Ted. I want to see that rock more closely. The last time we went, we just looked at the boat and did not notice the black rock at all. "Where did you see the other skeleton and what was its condition"?

"He was near a black rock and his arm was tied," Ted said. "How"?

"Maybe we found something there," John said. Maybe that part is the solution to our puzzle. "Did you look closely there"?

"Exactly not," Ted said. Because when I saw the skeleton, my attention was drawn to it and I went to it to see if I could find anything there; "I did not go around him anymore".

"How about Sarah?" John said.

"I do not think so," Ted said. "Sarah was very confused and did not look around".

"So we'd better go there tomorrow," John said. I think with all the enthusiasm that the professor has; As soon as possible, he will finish the work of that tablet; "So we have to do our job as quickly as possible".

"Maybe that stone tablet is the solution to this puzzle," Ted said. "Isn't it better to wait until professor translates the tablet?

"But I want to take a closer look before that," John said.

"So talk to Sarah tonight," Ted said. And they re-examined those pieces. John still did not understand the meaning of that light and was afraid to try it again; "Because he did not feel good about it".

John reached for the white orb so that he might be able to unravel its mystery. He held the orb in his hand and moved it in his hands. "Can you give me that?" Ted said to John.

Ted, as if something had caught his attention, took the orb and looked at it closely, saying, "There is a hole inside this that I do not know what it is and how it was created!" "Because I do not see any seams or cracks in the outer wall of the orb"?

"Well, of course," John said. "They did it when it was made".

"But what you are saying is possible now," Ted said. If this is an old object, I do not think it was possible to make such a thing then. "What do you think"?

"You are right," John said.

"Do you want to take a picture of it from ancient times to see what it was like and what was inside?" Ted said.

"It's a good idea," John said. OK; "What year should we consider"?

"I say, let's start three hundred years ago," Ted said.

John took the picture, but there was nothing in the picture. "Well, maybe three hundred years ago, this orb didn't exist," he told Ted.

"You'd better take a picture of the present," Ted said. And John took another picture and there was still nothing in the picture. "Maybe the camera is broken," John said. "I'd better take a photo from somewhere else." And he took a picture from the front view and the photo printed showed fifty years ago. "The camera is ok, but it can't be photographed," John said.

When John did not conclude, he left it and threw it on the ground. He searched his bag to find another device and thought about it. And he touched the diamond and took it out. When he took out the diamond and placed it in the sunlight, the rays of light coming out of the diamond gave a special beauty to the room.

"It's so beautiful," Ted said. "When you see it, you are fascinated by it".

"Oh, there's a dazzling light that draws you to it," John said.

Ted and John looked at the surrounding wall; to the light playing in diamonds and light moving; it was as if the waves were moving on the wall.

"These pictures on the wall are so much like that rock," Ted said.

"The more we think about that rock and that place, the image of it is more evocative," John said.

Ted shouted and pointed to the ground. John looked at the spot Ted was pointing to and noticed that the white orb was suspended between the ground and the air. John wanted to touch the orb, but the heat of the ball burned his hand and he moved away from the orb. John lowered the diamond and the orb came closer to the diamond. He dropped the diamond, and the diamond and the orb were both suspended between the ground and the air, and the diamond was placed inside the ball for a few seconds and fell to the ground. And this was the second weird scene John and Ted had seen in those two days; it was still hard to believe!

"All of these devices that are here are related, and we just have to figure out how they relate to each other and that if it works for us at all," John said.

Ted was still surprised and did not know what had happened. That night, at dinner, professor was very happy, and after dinner, John said to Sarah, "If possible, I want to go to sea again tomorrow".

"How interesting," Sarah said. I also wanted to go to sea together tomorrow; "Because I don't work tomorrow".

Professor jumped in between them and said, "Children, I want to give you some important news; I have finished translating that tablet and I think it is better to read it before going to sea; "Because it works for you a lot".

All three said, "Is it over"?

"I mean, it's so soon," John said.

"As if you did not want it to end soon!" Said professor. "Well, anyway, I'm done it".

"No, Professor," I said, "I did not expect you to finish it so soon!" Oh, that previous text took longer; "Well, what is written on that tablet, which is so important"?

Professor went to his room and brought a piece of paper with him

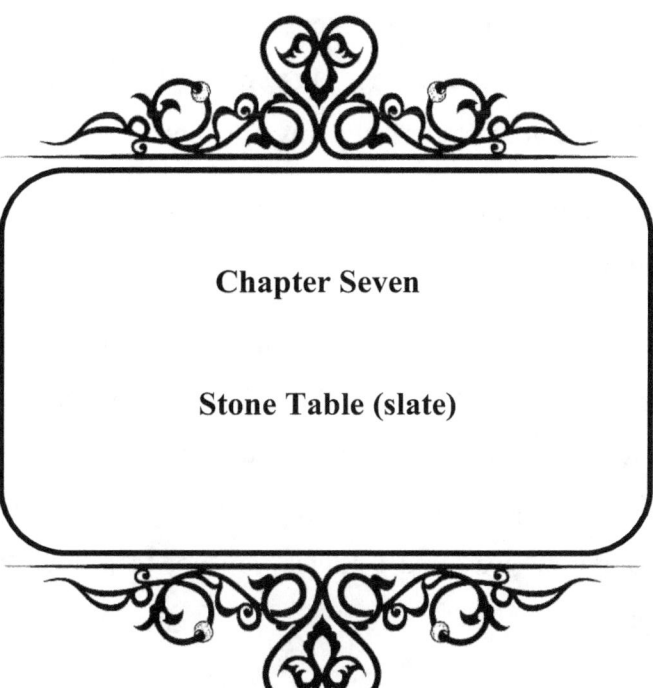

Chapter Seven

Stone Table (slate)

"O you who come to this place! Be aware that you step on a path that is difficult to cross. There are guiding and adviser lights in your path and misleading lights. Do not be greedy for the property of this palace which belongs to another.

The red earth and the green sky will be the means of misguidance; Take your steps slowly and keep your eyes open so that blackness does not swallow you. The birds sing and invite you; Do not step towards them.

I, the great John Wilson, paved the way for you; "May you continue my path."

When the text of the letter was finished, everyone looked at John and the professor said, "This letter must have been written by your grandfather; like the previous letter."It is not clear which path he is talking about, but whatever it is, it is a dangerous way and I advise you not to follow that path anymore."

"I came so far to discover the mystery of this path, and I cannot go back without finding the end of this path," John said. I do not ask you to come with me, but I will go; "I have to see where it's written in the letter!"

"I will never leave you alone," Ted said. "I will be with you until the end."

"Do whatever you think is right," the professor said. I will not hinder your work. I'm old enough for adventures like this and I'm not capable. "I do not know what Sarah thinks."

"I want to go with John and Ted," Sarah said. "While I was researching here, I came across a lot of strange things, and my experience can help them."

The next morning, they went to the desired point. Contrary to what he said last night, the professor had already prepared and was waiting for the rest. Ted, John, and Sarah were happy that the professor's decision had been changed, and they smiling headed for the black rock. John had put everything he had found in the bag. After reading that tablet (slate), John was more purposeful to discover a new way that day. After jumping into the water, they went to the Black Rock. John asked Ted where the skeleton was found and they went there together. All three were looking for something unusual at different points. John went to the part of the Black Rock where the skeleton was. John believed that whatever should be, is inside the rock. So he looked for the entrance to the rock and carefully examined the points of the rock.

After a few moments, Sarah approached John and showed him the seafloor. John noticed that there was a flat surface in a part of the seafloor that leads to the Black Rock. It seemed that something have been drawn on it. John carefully cleaned it and saw a red line on the seafloor. John followed that line.

The end of that line leads to the Black Rock. John guesses that the entrance to the palace, written on a stone tablet, must be here, and goes to the Black Rock and searches every point on it. In one part of the rock, he found a special hole that seemed to have been created by hand and was not natural. When Sarah saw that John was working hard to find a way to get into the Black Rock, he went and continued her search. After Sarah left, Ted reached out to John and opened his fist; a light shone from his hand; John took it and put it in his bag. John looked down at the rock and noticed a phosphorescent light there. He cleared the mud and silts on it and followed that line and reached the first point again. That line indicated the boundary of the Black Rock.

It had been a few hours since they had gone into the water; Sarah came to John and asked him to go to the water surface. Sarah felt weak and tired. When John saw Sarah in that state, he thought it best to return to the surface to rest and eat, and after reaching the boat, they saw the professor waiting for them; Of course, after rising from the water, he complained a little about why they came so late.

After some rest and food and the usual talk of what was going on underwater and explaining the story to the professor, John asked to go into the cabin to examine the tools he had found and to investigate their connection. They went into the cabin and John took out the light object that Ted had found and examined it again, but he did not notice anything. The white orb caught his attention again and he picked it up and turned it in his hand. He felt that the surface of the orb matched the hole of the rock. "I think this orb is for the hole of the rock, and we have to put it in that part," John said. "I think something new will happen with this orb."

They were thinking that the doorbell rang and Sarah's voice was heard from behind the door, "John, don't you want to go underwater again?"

"Of course, we're coming," John said. And then he put all the things in the bag and they went under the water. John went back to the black rock to put his thoughts into action. As soon as he reached the black rock, he took the orb out of the bag and put it in the hole of the rock. The orb was placed exactly in its place, but nothing happened on the rock. Seeing that nothing special was happening, John wanted to pick up the orb, but all his efforts were useless. The orb does not move. Ted, who was watching John's efforts from a distance, approached him and asked him what was going on. John explained to Ted that the orb would not move.

"I think the orb is back in its place," Ted said. "Like that diamond that did not come apart when it was inserted into the orb."

"Then why didn't something happen?" John said. "I thought that now the rock should be split and we could see inside the rock and enter, but nothing happened."

John felt frustrated that his thought had not been put into practice and that what was in his head had not happened. "This orb should indeed be here," Ted said. We must do other things to be able to open the door. We have to look for a solution. We came about 50 percent of the way; we can go the rest of the way and find the way. "John comes on, let's go again."

When Sarah heard them, she came to them and said, "What are you talking about?" And John explained to Sarah.

They did not conclude that day and returned to the surface to search with more energy tomorrow. That night, Ted and John in their room re-examined the items they had found and, as usual, fell asleep without much success. That night, Ted dreamed that they were submerged again, and while

John was wandering around the rock, a black light from the rock dragged John and while Ted made every effort it was impossible to make John realize this. He tries to swim towards John, but something seems to grab Ted's legs and does not allow him to swim. Ted starts screaming in his sleep, but his voice is lost in the waves. ...

Ted woke up with the sound of John shaking his shoulders. His face was wet. John brought a glass of water for Ted. After drinking water, Ted explained his dream to John. John thought for a moment and said, "I do not know what this dream can mean! Does it make sense at all? Or maybe it's because of being in that point; "Anyway, hopefully, nothing bad will happen to us." And they slept again.

The next morning, they went to the same place again; the same rock underwater. John moved to the rock, and Ted, with the dream he had had the night before, had decided to walk with John only that day and would not leave him. "Don't worry," said John. Nothing happens to me; "I am aware of my surroundings."

"No, it's better," Ted said. "If something is to happen, we will both be together." John was convinced, and this time they both went to the top of the rock together, where something might be found. When they reached the top, there was nothing strange on the rock. Sarah, at the bottom of the rock, was watching. Something seemed to be catching her eye. After clearing the seafloor of some mud, she found something and when she saw it, she quickly reached them and they quickly got to that point. What Sarah had found was like a hatch and had something like a handle. John tried to pull the handle, but his effort was useless.

"I don't think it could be opened by hand," Sarah said. "We need leverage to open it." So they went to the surface; both to catch their breath and to find something they can open that hatch.

Professor was still waiting for new news and was impatient. Sarah told him everything that happened underwater. "I do not think that hatch can be opened with leverage," professor said; "Given that the hatch, which has not been opened for several years, has probably taken up a lot of sediment and requires more force to open it."

"It's better to try with the leverage first," John said. "If not, we will think of another way to open it." And they went under the water again. As the professor had said, opening that hatch was not easy. After a useless attempt, they returned to the surface. Professor, when saw their faces, noticed the matter and said, "Sarah, does this boat have a crane?" "Yes, but its chain is not long enough to reach that depth," Sarah said.

"Can't you find a shipping company to do that?" John said.

"I do not think so," Sarah said. But... "And then she continued:" There is a friend of mine who I think has something that will benefit us. I have to talk to him; "I hope he still has it."

They returned home, and Sarah called her friend without delay, and a few minutes later, with a smile, she left her room and said, "It looks like something can be done." "Stephen had a hand crane that we used to use when we were looking for lost objects underwater," she explained. He has not used it for a long time now; "When we saw that nothing could be found on the island, we set it aside."

"So be careful not to Draw attention when you try to get the crane from Stephen," John said.

After a short rest, Sarah went to her friend and returned with the crane a few hours later, saying, "Fortunately, it is still working."I hope it has the power to push that hatch out of its place."

Night at bedtime, Ted said, "I feel that what we were looking for; that is the entrance to the Black Rock, is under that hatch."What do you think?"

"I was thinking the same thing," John said. "We have to wait until tomorrow." The next day, they all went back to that point of the sea with that hand crane. Sarah stood right on top of the rock; given the exact coordinates had given to her by John. This time, Sarah did not go under; because she knew how to work with a crane. John and Ted went underwater. John threw the hook cable hardly to the hatch handle due to sediments on the handle. Of course, he did that after a little effort and scraping the sediments.

The crane started working. At first, no matter what it pulls, the hatch does not move. "Wait a minute," Ted said, then came to the surface and took the lever from Sarah and went to the hatch. He tapped the hatch slightly so that the sediments might loosen, hooked the lever into the handle, and then asked Sarah to try again. Sarah turned on the device and John and Ted pushed the lever at the same time. The hatch shook a little, but still, they were not strong enough to lift the hatch. "Sarah, try again," Ted said. They pushed again with maximum force and the hatch went up a bit, but it fell again. "Let's try again, but this time, as soon as we get up, we have to put something under it," Ted said. "Do you see anything around here?"

John looked around and picked up the piece of flat stone and said, "What do you think of this?"

"I think it's good," he said. Let's try again and then he told Sarah again that we would try again. Sarah turned on the device, and they pressed the lever at the same time, and after rising a little, John immediately put the stone under the door. Ted asked Sarah to hold the device in the same position, then looked for the larger piece of stone, placed it painfully near the hatch, and then asked Sarah to move the crane again. After the hatch had risen slightly, Ted placed a larger rock under the hatch and asked Sarah to do the same thing again, and finally, the hatch opened completely.

Inside the pit under the valve was metal-like leverage. John stepped forward and pulled the lever, but again what John expected did not happen.

John was frustrated that he was doing everything he could, to get what he wanted, but there was nothing. John stood still, thinking that he had at once put his hand inside his bag, pulled out a luminous object, and hurried to the black rock. John swam to a part of the Black Rock where he had found another hole. He placed a luminous stone in that hole and the rock shook and the earth around it began to shake in the same way. When Ted saw the shaking of the black rock, he remembered his dream and immediately swam to John to reach him. The phosphor line around the Black Rock began to rotate. As John stared at the black rock, John realized that the line had rotated seven times and then stopped, and the black rock was cracking; the crack was getting deeper and deeper. After the rock cracked and opened, a stream of water began to flow from the inside of the rock into it. The power of the stream was gradually increasing. Ted realized that John was overwhelmed by what was happening. Remembering what he had dreamed, Ted tried to take John away, but it was as if John was traveling in another world; because whatever Ted shook him and wanted to take with him was not possible. After Ted's useless efforts, Sarah, hearing the sound of the black rock shaking, reached out to them and went to Ted, and together they tried to lift John, but it was as if John was clinging to the ground. The intensity of the flow was much greater; As Sarah and Ted were drawn to it. It seemed that John was no longer floating in the water and was moving in the direction of the flow. Realizing that they could not carry John with them, Ted and Sarah took John by the hand so that they could join him. John approached the black rock. He could see in his mind that

Sarah and Ted were trying to hold him, but a force seemed to be blocking their movement toward the Black Rock. John was fully aware of what was happening around him. When they reached the entrance to the rock, there were steps at the entrance that continued into the rock. John stepped on the first step and climbed it; from the first step to the last step, there were seven steps and the distance between the steps was long. At the top of the stairs was a large door that all parts of the door were covered with gold. There were shiny diamonds that gleamed in the eye. When they reached the top of the stairs, John had control over his feet. Looked around well; He was looking for a way to open that door. He thought that to open the door, there must be another hole in the wall around the door; so he went up and down to find it. Ted and Sarah were surprised by John's behavior. Meanwhile, Sarah pushed lightly on the entrance, and a voice came from the door and began to move. Hearing the sound of the door, John stopped in his tracks and turned his attention to the door. Three were staring at the door; Seconds later, John and Ted pushed themselves against the door, this time pushing the three together. It opened a little and they were able to enter; the first person that entered was John. Ted was careful that John did not distance himself from him. So after John, Ted came in, and then Sarah. The space behind the door was dark. Sarah turned on her flashlight and got closer to John to see the way better. They had not walked a few steps when Ted felt something pass them by. They were moving in an obscure, vague, and dark direction in flashlight; without seeing anything. John wanted to get to what was on the stone tablet, and he knew it had to be the gate to the castle in question. Something could be seen in the distance, in which darkness shone, and its light had caught John's attention. So he hurried to the light that had been emitted from the lightning, but when he reached that point he found nothing special.

It had been almost ten minutes since they had been on the move; John stood up and, without a word, took the flashlight from Sarah and turned on their backs. In disbelief, they saw that they were where they entered through the door, and only a few steps away from the door. Sarah was scared of this and said, "How is it possible!"We have been moving forward for almost ten minutes now."

After a long silence, John said, "Nothing is moving here at all; we felt we were moving forward."I doubted it after the first few minutes, but I could not believe it."

John handed the flashlight to Sarah and asked her to shine it on the bag. He took the black object and the metal plate out of the bag, found a flat spot on the floor, and placed the metal plate on it. He put a black object on it carefully. The same thing happened like in the room, and the object began to spin, and a great deal of light came from it; So that it illuminated the whole space. This time more light was emitted from the object. When all the darkness was completely gone, John looked around. There seemed to be creatures moving around that John could not identify.

Chapter Eight

Entering the Unknown Corridor

John was looking for a way to go, or if there was any way they could get rid of it. John realized that the space they were in was no bigger than a 7x7 room with seven doors, each of which probably ended up somewhere. John moved to the first door and examined it carefully. On that door was a lock that needed a key to open it. John knew those locks could no longer be opened by the force of arm and must have been the key to unlocking them. He looked at the other doors; all seven doors were similar. John reached into his bag to try the key he had already found on the door. There was one recess in each of the seven doors, all of which were black. John started from the first door to his left and put the key in the door and turned it to the right, but the key did not move. He went to the next door and it did not open. In the same way, he tried all the doors and none of them opened until he reached the seventh door; He turned the key and this time the door opened. With a push on the door, the door opened completely. The other side of the door was dark and nothing could be seen. John took the flashlight from Sarah and turned it into the darkness inside the back door, but still, nothing was clear. John turned to them and said, "Very well, guys ... we have come this far together; It is not clear what will happen next and where we will go. I want to go the rest of the way, behind this door. I do not know what is waiting for me there. I ask you to return to the surface of the water. This is my story and I do not want anyone to be harmed by my curiosity; "Anyway, if something happens to me, no one is waiting for me and no one is worried about me, but you are different."

Ted looked into John's eyes and said, "What did you think of me?" I always told you, this is the way we started together and we will finish it together. "I do not know Sarah, but I will come with you."

"I would like to come with you," Sarah said. I do not think behind the door is a danger; because this rock, itself, pulls us here and I want to see what the end of it is! "I have been to more dangerous places before."

John was overjoyed that his friends did not leave him alone, and said, "Well, now that you want, I have nothing to say and I will be happy."

John went to the black object and the metal plate and put them in the bag. When the black object was removed, the light disappeared and in the same darkness, it moved towards them again, and then all three entered the dark corridor.

At the very beginning of the journey, John removed the key from the door so that he could open it if it came back and the door was closed. When the three of them entered, as soon as they took the first step, Ted's foot rested on something that caused the door to close behind them firmly.

"Okay, I picked up the key," John said.

By saying this, John was trying to alleviate the fear in his friends. In that darkness, they were moving carefully and slowly. Ted asked John to use that light again to get to know their surroundings better, and John welcomed the idea and re-created the light using a metal plate and a black object. The corridor was lit, but the end was still dark. He glanced around and counted the width of the corridor with his footsteps; it was seven. There was nothing special on the walls. He looked at the ground and found a button on the wall ahead. He pressed that button and heard a sound like draining water. After a while, the water level inside the corridor went down and after thirty minutes, the water was completely drained. They took out all three oxygen capsules and a mask and took a deep breath.

"It's so much better this way," Ted said.

"Yes, but we do not know if we will need them or not," said Sarah. "Isn't it better to take these with us?"

"Oh no," said John. It is very heavy. It stops us from moving. "It's better to leave these here and take it back when we're backing ..." Sarah considered John's words logical and accepted it.

"What do we do with this one now?" Ted said.

"What's the problem?" Said, John.

"The light, as you can see at the end of the corridor, is dark again, and it shows that this is a long way and that we cannot hold this metal plate in our hands and walk," Ted said. "Now what do you think we should do?"

"You're right," John said. There must be something else on the wall; "Just as a button for draining water for lighting must be something."

"Unless the creatures that live here do not need light," Ted said.

"You mean, what creatures?" Said Sarah, who was frightened.

"I do not know," Ted said. Anything can be here; like the creature, we saw in the previous room. "Have you ever seen a creature like that?"

"No," Sarah said.

"Well ... you saw them swimming without light," Ted said. It must be the same again; isn't that right??

"Yes, you are right," Sarah replied fearfully.

John realized that Sarah was scared and said, "I do not think anything scary is waiting for us. You saw that the creature had nothing to do with us. "Instead, we should find a way to light here."

"Can't we use a flashlight?" Sarah said.

"The flashlight is dim, and then we do not know how long it will last," John said. And then he went to the surrounding wall to find a way to light it there. John wanted to search the wall as clearly as possible. He turned to Ted and said, "You and Sarah look at the wall on the other side; "Maybe you found something."

Sarah and Ted checked the wall. After a bit of searching and walking, a part of the wall caught John's attention. The color of that part was different from the other parts. It was as if they had changed the wall or it was a sign. He hit it with his hand; it was as if the sound that was heard from that part was different from other places; the back of it seemed to be empty. John repeated this several more times. Ted and Sarah, who had not found anything themselves, noticed John and went to the sound that John had made. "I think there is something," John turned to Ted. "We must try to remove this tile."

"Let me try," Ted said. He tapped the tile and then looked around. He used the knife he had hidden in his diving bag, scraped around the tile, and then gently struck it so that the tile would not break. Ted took the flashlight from Sarah to see the back of the tile. He turned the light towards that part. There was an empty tile behind it. "Nothing is behind it," Ted said after seeing it there. John took the flashlight from Ted to see. John did not find anything. Sarah approached John and said, "Let me see there too." And he gave the flashlight to Sarah. Ted and John felt frustrated and continued to search without waiting for Sarah's opinion. Moments later, Sarah said, "John ... I think there is something; "Can you come and see?" "What?" John said in surprise. "I did not see anything!"

"Come for a moment," Sarah said. "You can see by yourself."

John and Ted walked to Sarah. "Do you see that hole?" Sarah said. "It looks like something is there."

John asked Sarah to bring the light closer to that part, and as the light approached, the hole became apparent, and he said to Sarah, "Yes, you are right; "But what?"

"Maybe like that door, we have to put something in," Ted said. "Look, is there anything else between your tools for there?"

"I do not think so," John said. "Because it has a special shape."

Ted reached out to them and asked the two to show him the hole, and after seeing what Sarah and John had seen, he continued, "I think there is something to match here from the things I found. » "What do you think it's for?" He said to John.

"Have you ever noticed that everything here is seven?" Sarah said. Seven doors, 7× 7 rooms, and this special shape that has seven sides! "Do you think that having seven things here is a special sign?"

John, who liked Sarah's attention, said, "Well done Sarah! I had not paid attention to this issue until now. "There were seven steps at the entrance."

"Yeah, but you think the number seven helps solve our problem," Ted said. "I mean light here."

"Maybe it will help," John said. "Maybe not."

"I hope we can find a solution to this," Ted said. "I do not want our work to end here."

"It's better to keep searching," John said. "Maybe we will find something." And he went to the wall and began to search. Sarah and Ted returned to their former place. John touched the wall again and examined it carefully. Suddenly he remembered the camera and took it out of his diving backpack and went to the tile and took a picture of it, but the output of the picture showed nothing. He repeated the taking photo from the wall several more times, but to no avail. The camera did not work there. When he put the camera inside the bag, his eyes fell on the necklace which had come out from the skeleton. He picked it up and looked at it well and carefully; He pulled the stone out of its place and shouted for joy ... Ted and Sarah ran towards him with a shout of joy and happiness.

"What happened?" Ted said.

"I think I found it," John said.

"What did you find?" Sarah said.

"The thing we have to put there, on that hole ..." John said.

"Where is it from?" Ted said. "Was it on the wall?"

"No, do you remember the necklace I took from that skeleton neck?" Said, John.

"Yeah, I remember," Ted said.

"I took out the stone from that necklace and found that the stone was exactly the shape of that hole," John said.

"Well, why are you waiting?" Ted said. "Let's get to its place to get to work."

John put the stone in the hole, and after a few moments, the whole corridor lit up. "We finally solved this puzzle," said Sarah, who was overjoyed by the light. And all three laughed happily.

John picked up the black object and the metal plate and put them in the bag, and the three of them moved in the direction marked in red.

John, Ted, and Sarah had almost reached the end of the corridor. The end of the corridor reached the spring. They went to the spring to drink its water; when they reach the spring, a light shines from the bottom of the spring; it was as if that spring was full of light. First of all, John stepped forward to get some water; as he approached the spring, the

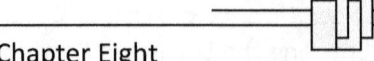
light emanating from the spring and the face of the man he had seen in his dream appeared. John went back in fear and got stuck in a rock and fell...

Chapter Nine

Move to the Dream Place

"What's the matter?" Ted asked as John fell to the ground.

"Look at that light," John said. "What I see, do you see?"

Ted and Sarah looked at the light and said, "Did you have an illusion??" "There is nothing there!"

John looked again; it was as if they were right; there was nothing there. "Yes, you are right," John said. "I felt like I saw a man's face in that light."

"I'd better get some water," Ted said. "You are tired." And he approached the spring. The same thing happened to Ted, and he said in surprise, "You were right; "I see a man's face."

"Yeah," said John, it was the face of the man I had dreamed of! Suddenly, a voice said, "Hello John."You have finally reached this point ..."

After hearing that sound, all three shouted, and then the laughing sound of that image was heard. John asked the man, "Who are you?" How do you know me? "I saw you in a dream."

"Yes, John, I'm Andreas Bellini," the image said. I've been seeing you all this time while you were searching for here. I was the one who put that black stone in the dumpster so that you come here. I knew that you are an intelligent boy and you can find your way and endure all these hardships. I am Andreas Bellini and an old friend of your ancestors, and your grandfather entrusted me with something to entrust to someone worthy of his family. All these years I knew all the members of your family, but none of them deserved to receive this trust. But when I saw you, I realized that you could be that person; that's why I left these signs for you to see if you can get to the point and you were lucky enough to get there, but this is just the beginning, and after that, you have to go through a winding path. Here you will encounter things that you have never seen before and you have to cross paths that you will encounter unexpected scenes; if you can get through all these steps safely, I'm waiting behind this path; "I hope to see you there."

Before John could say anything or ask another question, the image faded and all three were stunned. After the image disappeared, a package came on the water. John noticed the package and picked it up. The package looked like a map. Ted picked it up and they looked at it with Sarah.

"We'd better get water from here," John said. We may be thirsty on the way. I wish we had something to eat; "I feel hungry."

John was saying these words when some fruit and food came up to the water and John, happy with what he had got, went into the water and took them all and divided them. He put some in his waist bag and gave some to Ted and Sarah. They rested a bit before leaving to have enough energy to go the way Andreas had mentioned. After some sleep and rest, they were ready to go.

John, Sarah, and Ted set out on a journey that did not know what was going to happen to them, but a curiosity to understand the end of the road led them to take this winding road and continue until the end. The path was not dark anymore and they had no problem with the light. They seemed to be walking for an hour. "It's better to take a closer look at the map and see which way we're going," John said.

"Of course, if we can figure it out," Ted said.

"I'd better sit here and relax and see the map," John said. And then he sat down before the others and opened the map and examined it carefully. "Look here, Ted," John said. This map shows where we are now. "I think the light you see on the map will be us."

"Yeah, well," Ted said, "but now how do we know where to go?"

"I think our destination is here," John pointed to part of the map. He pointed to a place on the map that was a castle and continued: "If we pay attention to this map, we will not deviate from the path; "Because it shows us that we are moving in the right direction."

After a while, they rested and, happy that they had read the map, continued on their way.

The route they took was full of high and short mountains. A few hours after walking, they felt tired again and decided to rest, so they sat down on a mountain, part of which was flat and they could sit. John took out the food and fruit he had taken from the water and shared them with his friends. Sarah was engrossed in her thoughts and ate in the world of thought and reflection; Seeing Sarah's condition, John said, "What are you thinking?"

Sarah came to her senses and said, "Oh ...! Nothing; Honestly, I was thinking about the number seven. Like I said before, everything here is seven. It has occupied my mind a lot; "There must be a reason!"

"I do not think so," Ted said. Any other number could be instead of seven. "Do not complicate matters too much."

"So far, what the number seven is about," Sarah said. Did you hear?"

"No, I did not hear anything," Ted said.

"I have heard that the number seven is sacred in some religions or countries, but I do not know why," John said.

"So far," Sarah said, "you have noticed that the wonders of the world are seven, or that the gods of ancient Greece, for example, were seven gods, or that the sky had seven floors, or that heaven and hell, according to the religions, had seven floors, and there are seven musical notes! Do you think this is all a coincidence? There is also a story about the number seven, which was compiled and published in a book in 1889. This story is about the method of counting among a tribe, which used only the words "one" and "two" to count. For example, instead of the number three, it says "two and one", instead of four, it says "two and two", instead of five, it says "two and two and one" and for the number six, it says "two, two, two". , But for numbers greater than six, they said "very much." This can be the beginning of the formation of numbers in the first human life. And because the number seven was unknown to them, the number was known as sacred. When the Egyptians and Babylonians identified the five planets closest to the sun, they added the moon and the sun to the five planets, bringing them to seven. There are many other things about the number seven; For example the seven great sins, the last seven words of Jesus, the seven humanities, the seventh heaven, the seventh "S" of the Iranian Nowruz, and many other cases ... Why do you think the person who built this room focused so much on the number seven? Mark everything with the number seven. Don't you think there is a secret behind this choice? "Or did not he/she want to point us out?"

"Surely the number seven was sacred to this man, like the tribes you mentioned," Ted said.

"Yes, it is possible," Sarah said. "But my mind is very much involved and I feel I have to find a connection between them."

"I also think the number seven is sacred to the builder of this building, and for that reason, he denoted everything by seven," John said.

Sarah shrugged her shoulders and raised her eyebrows in confusion. After eating and resting, they decided to continue on their way. They packed up the objects and put them in a bag. John opened the map and looked at it again so that they would not go the wrong way, and after seeing the map, they moved on. There was a stream on their way, which seemed very strange. The water flow was opposite to the stream path and upwards. The flow of water caught John's attention, and he said to Sarah, "Did you notice that the water is upward?"

Sarah looked at the water and said, "We are seeing strange things here, but I did not see that!"

"If we want to spend our time solving the puzzles here, I think we'll spend a year here without results," Ted said. It is better to continue on the path; "Because there are so many weird things like that."

Sarah and John confirmed Ted's words and kept moving. After crossing the difficult path, they reached a high level where the water stream reached that point. It was weirder than before. The water flowed to a flat place where it was not clear how the water sank, and more interestingly, up there were fish that moved in the air without water, and only moved to the extent that the mountain walls continued. , and turned back again. Rainbow-colored fish were on that side of the mountain, connecting the two rainbow-like mountains like a bridge. At the top of the mountain was an old weeping willow tree, the branches of which reached to the ground, and beneath the tree grew inverted tulips that gave it a unique beauty.

"We'd better take a break and review the map," John said after their eyes got a little accustomed to the strange environment and the intensity of their surprise reduced. And with Sarah and Ted's agreement, they sat down under the willow tree. Ted took the container of water to fill it with water flowing in the stream, and John spread the map on the ground so he could see it. Seeing the map, Sarah said, "It seems that we have reached the right path, but this castle on the map is behind the second mountain; Of course, it seems that there is a distance between the mountain and the castle, it is not known how long it will take and what other things are waiting for us, but the problem we are facing at the moment is the distance between the two mountains. I looked down and could not see anything but darkness, but it can be said that the way down the mountain is almost smooth and we cannot go down from there, or at least it is very difficult and requires mountaineering equipment and people who have done this before; It is only after going down this mountain and along with the distance between the two mountains that from this top and in this darkness it is not clear what is happening there. "We have to climb the second mountain, which is also smooth and impassable to pass, "Let's go up and see what happens next on the mountain!"

Ted said after Sarah's talk: "Well ... with these words you want to make us realize that it is no longer possible to continue and we have to go back? I must say right now that I did not come all this way to go back with a little problem. I'm with John to the end of the path, and nothing is holding me back; "Unless John wants to come back, I don't think John has that opinion either."

Ted turned to John and looked at John, waiting for his confirmation. Realizing what Ted meant, John looked at Sarah and said, "I do not think anyone who has taken us to this point of the path would expect us to go down this mountain." "I am sure there is a way or a crossing or a bridge to cross this path." And then he turned to Ted and said, "Ted, thank you for always helping me, but I don't think Sarah means we're going back." Sarah was explaining the way forward so that we could think of a solution for it. "Certainly she did not endure so much hardship to come here." And then he turned to Sarah, and Sarah nodded in approval of John's words, saying, "I like you and Ted, would love to see the end of this story where it ends. I'm looking for a way to get to that mountain. "Do you have an idea to cross here?"

"I do not know," said Ted, who was a little relieved. "Maybe we should climb over this rainbow and reach that mountain ourselves."

Sarah blinked with joy and said, "Why not! Isn't everything weird here? This is definitely why this rainbow is here too ... weren't we looking for a bridge to cross? "I do not think there is a problem with trying it."

"Yeah," Ted said. But you thought that if you set foot on it and there is nothing that can support your weight and then you fall, what will happen? »That means the end of the journey. "

"I do not think anyone must stand on it," John said. "By putting something on the rainbow, we can try it."

John was looking for a piece of stone to place on the rainbow bridge. He found a piece of stone and placed it on the rainbow bridge, and in despair, the stone fell to the bottom of the mountain. All three sighed in despair and regret. "Maybe there's a lever ... something around that, by pulling it, will create a bridge for us to cross," Sarah said again. "Let's take a good look around together." And first of all, she started the search. John and Ted also searched, but the further they went, the less they concluded. After finding no way to build a bridge, all three sat on the ground, tired and thirsty. Sarah lay on the floor with her hands under her head. John leaned against the tree and stared at the map so he might find a way. Ted was drawing geometric shapes on the floor with a piece of wood in his hand. And all three, for a moment, quietly drowned in their thoughts. "Why is there no sky here?" Sarah said as she looked up. Do you think there is no day or night here? Sun, moon, and stars! "I do not see any of this!"

"Well ... of course ... we're miles underwater," Ted said. "It should not be the sky."

"There should be no land or mountains," Sarah said.

"Ted did not say anything when he realized that Sarah was right and that such a place under the water was strange."

"This time the solution must be something else," Sarah said. "The further we go, the harder the solution becomes."

"That's right," John said as he looked at the map. "I was happy with Ted's idea about the Rainbow Bridge, and I thought it was right that it was a rainbow bridge, but unfortunately, our guess was wrong."

"John, do you think that stuff in the bag doesn't help us?" Ted said.

John looked at Ted and then hurried to the bag and emptied it on the floor. He was looking for something that could solve this problem. Sarah and Ted calmed down and helped John find the right object, but it was in vain. John explored every way he could think of to find a solution in his mind; He even looked for rocks so that he might build a bridge on the rock, but he did not find anything like that. After a useless attempt, all three sat down again in despair. With Ted's help, John collected the items and carefully and obsessively put them in the bag in the order he had in mind.

"It's better to eat a little to make our minds work better," said Sarah, who was lying down again. Maybe we will find a solution; By the way, we are on the move for a long time; "We'd better get some sleep."

John and Ted agreed with Sarah. After eating, they slept under the weeping willow tree in the thicket of tulips and other fragrant flowers that had grown there; Deep sleep.

John dreamed of his childhood playing with Ted. The day Ted bought a lot of balloons to fly the rabbit they had found. And after inflating the balloons and tying the rabbit to it, the poor white rabbit, without wings, flew; Of course, they also had a rope in their hand that they could control and pull down, but due to the strong wind and the rapid movement of the balloons, Ted and John were forced to run, and Ted got stuck in a stone and fell to the ground. John's white rabbit soared into the air with the balloons, and John's never to see it again. John opened his eyes and saw the leaves of the weeping willow tree above his head as if moving. The wind seemed to be blowing. John got up, and after looking around to find the source of the wind, he went to the water stream and splashed water on his face. He sat down by the water and stared at the part where the water sank to the ground. John was looking for something in that part of the earth that the water stream was leading to. He found a piece of wood and went to the place where the water sank into the ground and because whatever was dug up, it was replaced again, and the soil that he had dug up and dumped in another part would sink to the ground. John was tired of doing this and moved to the tree. Ted was almost awake and Sarah was waking up. When Sara woke up, she rubbed her eyes and said, "How many hours do you think we slept?"

"It's not clear," John said. Because all the electronic devices are out of order here. "It has happened since we entered the room."

"How interesting," Sarah said. "I did not pay attention to this issue at all." And then she went to the water stream and washed his hands and drank some water and returned to her place.

John turned to Ted and said, "Do you know what dream I had?" He waited for John to continue talking. "I had a dream about a rabbit that we sent into the air by tying it to a balloon," John continued.

Ted smiled and said, "Yeah, I think the poor animal fainted from fear. I remember you loved that rabbit very much. After the rope fell from my hand, you cried for two days and didn't talk to me; do you remember?"

"Yeah," said John, "oh my father bought that rabbit for my birthday; "That's why it was so important to me." And then he sighed with regret for the happy days and the loss of his family and became silent.

Ted, noticing John's condition, approached John and put his hand on John's shoulders, saying, "Do not be sad, and buddy! You have me who always watched over you. I have just found you and I will never leave you alone; "Even if you want to."

John put his hand on Ted's hand and thanked him. Seeing this scene, Sarah shed tears, but to change the atmosphere, she said, "What did you say you did to the poor rabbit?"

John smiled and replied, "Nothing ... we tied some balloons to it and sent it to fly." and then all three laughed.

After a little laugh and joke, Sarah moved towards the fish and started playing with them. After a while, she came back and said to John, "I have an idea; "If we can use the fish as balloons to make the rabbit fly and force it to move to the other side of the mountain, we can get to the point with them."

"Yeah, it's a good idea," said John, his eyes twinkling with hope.

"I just hope they can bear the weight of us," Ted said.

"We just have to see, we can divert them," Sarah said. "because they only move in one direction."

After Sarah's sentence, the three of them thought about finding a solution to the idea that Sarah had come up with.

"We'd better try first and try to divert one of the fish from its path," John said. And then he moved towards them. He picked one of the fish and tried to divert it, but the fish got angry and made a sound that the other fish attacked. Ted saw the scene and quickly got to that point, picking up John and taking him somewhere far away. But the fish followed them, to the point of John and Ted, and then stood still. It was clear that they were looking at John.

"If we knew the language of the fish, they probably wouldn't have told us good things," John said.

"Yeah, you're right," Ted said. And then they both laughed.

"You saw how sharp their teeth were," Sarah said. "I think they were preparing to bite."

"On this way, I must be very grateful to Ted for getting me out healthy of another battle," John said.

Ted blushed a little and scratched the back of his head, saying, "I told you I always watch over you."

John smiled and looked at Ted again to thank him, then said to Sarah, "I think we have to find another way to get the fish out of the way."

"Yes, that's right," Sarah said. "But what can take them elsewhere."

"If someone wants to trick me and drag me away, with food, he/she can do it very easily," Ted said. And then he put his hand on his stomach and continued, "Especially if I'm hungry." And he laughed. John took something out of his bag and said, "So we'd better eat something ourselves first and then think about what these fish like to eat to prepare for them."

"I think they like our meat more," Sarah smiled.

"Experience is a strict teacher," John said. Because it holds the exam first and then gives you the necessary lessons. "(Vernon) so we should try and learn the lessons in this story."

"Yeah, until we experience something, we can't figure out what's behind it," Ted said, eating with a full mouth. "Unless anyone else has experienced it before and we can use it."

Sarah looked at Ted and said, "Well done Ted!" "It was a beautiful sentence." "That's why the history teacher used to say that we should always learn from the past so that the mistakes they made, we will not do it again, but since I love the experience of new work, I did not accept these things; I have already said this to say that I also know about these things and I do not run out of him." John and Sarah laughed out loud, and Ted laughed at them. After eating and resting, John said, "Well, well; "Now what food do you think these beautiful fish like?"

"If their appetites are like my aquarium fish, they must love meat or worms or insects," Ted said. "Most fish eat things like this."

"Now where do we find these things?" John said.

"I think there are different insects on that tree or under the ground," Ted said. "So it's better to look at these two points first."

Ted went to the tree and John followed him. Ted turned the leaves of the tree and said to John, "You'd better look around." Dig the soil and turn it upside down; "Something will probably be found."

"What should I do?" Said Sarah.

"Come with me on these leaves, look for an insect that will benefit the fish," Ted said. After some searching, they found some insects and earthworms. "Ted, you better go-ahead to feed," John said. Because they do not have happy memories of me. "They may attack me again."

Ted grabbed the insect container and headed for the fish. He took a worm in his hand and held out his hand to one of the fish; the fish swallowed the worm very quickly and waited there for food again.

"Go to the rainbow so it goes out of bounds," John said. "Ted did the same, and the fish followed Ted and out of the rest of the fish ."

"It's great," John said. It works."

"These fish are belly like me," Ted said.

"Should we try the fish and see if they can tolerate our weight?" Said Sarah.

"How do we do that?" John said.

"If you hang on to it, it's clear," Sarah said.

John went the same way and did the same, but the fish could not bear the weight of John and came down. The fish made a sound again and went to the other fish.

"We have to use them all to bear our weight," Ted said. Like those balloons we tied to a rabbit; "The number of fish should be more."

John welcomed Ted's idea, saying, "We have to make a device that can carry all three of us together."That's why we need a rope to attach to the fish."

"I think we can use this willow tree here," Sarah said. And then he looked at Ted and waited for Ted to confirm his words.

Ted shook his head and said, "Yeah, that's a good idea; because at the moment there is nothing else around that we can use.''Let me see what can be done ... Anyway, my father is a mechanic and I worked alongside him and I'm more skilled in technical work than you."

"Yeah Ted, you better tell us to know what to do," Sarah said. "In this field, you are even stronger than us."

Ted blushed and shyly scratched the back of his head, then harrumphed, saying, "Uh oh ... well; "Let me see if we have anything with which we can cut these branches."

"You had a knife," John said. "Can't you do anything about it?"

"That knife is small and not strong enough to break branches," Ted said.

"You better use arm force," Sarah said.

Ted, who had gained more strength when he heard this, went to the tree, grabbed a branch of the tree, and tried to break it. It was a thin branch. Ted plucked the thin, thick branches from the tree by hand, sometimes with a knife, respectively. Then he said to John and Sarah, "I cut the thinner branches to use the rope and the rest to make the device to sit on."

It took about three hours to uproot the tree; one of the wonders of that tree was that every branch that Ted cut off was immediately replaced by another branch and grew. John was happy that they would not damage the tree and that the broken branches would be replaced quickly.

Hours passed and they were busy at the same place and did not think about time at all. After plucking the branches, they felt weak and tired, and Ted asked John to provide something to eat so that they could get ready to continue working after some rest and fresh energy. John took some of the things he had taken from the spring and told Ted, "This is almost the last meal that has left; "It is not much else."

"I'm not too upset," Ted said as he removed the pieces of food. "Because I know there will be food here."

Sarah was lying under the willow tree on the grass, staring up, smelling the apple in her hand. Meanwhile, a drop of water fell on Sarah's face, and a few moments later, the speed of the drops increased. The rain was so heavy that it was soon surrounded by a lake of raindrops, and the only land left was the land under the willow tree; because its height was higher than other places. The rain was so fast that in the first ten minutes, the lake appeared. It rained for about thirty minutes and stopped. Due to the accumulation of water and its collapse from the edge of the wall of the rock, a beautiful waterfall view was created...

"We were very lucky," Ted said. "Because if it had rained for another hour, I think we would have fallen with it." And then he turned to Sarah and said, "I think listening to you and wanting to show you that the sky is changing here." And then he smiled.

The rainwater was drained as quickly as it had been collected, and the ground returned to its original state; it was as if it had not rained at all.

"I do not know how many hours we have been here, but I'm so tired and I want to get some sleep," Ted said. I feel sleepy. "Let's realize that there is no day or night here." And all three slept.

After waking up, they began to make the equipment they needed to go to the second mountain. After four or five hours, the device they wanted was made. "If you weren't, I don't think I would have been able to make this device," John told Ted.

"That's nothing;" Ted said. "I did even bigger things."

"Well ... now how do we connect these to the fish?" Sarah said.

"I made a ring according to the number of fish," Ted said. "We throw them around the fish and sit inside the device ourselves."

"Well," said John. "How do we get the fish to cross our rainbow?"

"It is obvious," Ted said. With another meal ... »

"Yes, but how do we feed them to get them there," John said.

"Remember when we were kids," Ted said, "We saw a cartoon of a horseman riding a horse, and he could move it just by holding the carrot in front of the horse, and when the horse ate the carrot, it would not move."

"Yeah, I remember," Sarah said. It was an interesting cartoon. "I think it was a Donkey."

Ted smiled and said, "It doesn't matter much; I made something like this for each of the fish."We just have to find food for them and pray that it will work."

"And hopefully the fish will bear our weight," John said.

"Don't worry," Ted said. If they cannot bear the weight of all three of us, we die in pairs; I mean, I'm going with Sarah; I'll come back and pick you up; "I think it will be like this."

"It's a good idea," John said. Well done Ted! You are so smart."

"It's better to find food for these bellies than not eat ourselves," Ted said.

After finding the fish food and attaching it to the hook, the rings were thrown around the fish. Ted did this carefully so as not to frighten the fish, and then all three sat down in a basket, each holding two hooks and holding the hooks in front of the fish.

"Fortunately, they bore our weight," John said.

"Yeah, I'm not weight," Ted said. "I have no weight you are you are the heavier."

Seeing the prey, the fish moved, and as they moved toward the food, they moved toward the rainbow and above it. John saw the valley between the two rocks from above; "The end of the two rocks was nothing but darkness."

"It's so scary," Sarah said.

"Kids, beware of hooks," Ted said. "If it deviates, the fish will also deviate, and then it is not clear what will happen."

John confirmed Ted's words and looked straight ahead, holding the hook tightly so that nothing special would happen. It took about twenty minutes for them to cross the mountain. When they reached the other side, they got off and gave the prey to the fish, and released them. The view there was exactly like the first rock; a willow tree and the rest of the things that were on that side. The fish started moving like the other side.

"Very well," John said. It is better to move and put this device under the willow tree. "It will be necessary for us to return." And he moved ahead of Ted and Sarah. On the way, he saw circular stones hovering in the air, stepping down to a dark spot.

"I think we have to get down from here," John said. "I do not see any other way."

"Well," said Ted. So why are you waiting? "Let's go."

John stepped on the first step. The circular stone was unbalanced but had enough space to stand. John stood on the stone for a moment, and after a few moments, the rock moved down.

"Why are you waiting John?" Ted said. Jump on the next stone; "You should not stand on these stairs too much."

John immediately jumped on the next stone and the first stone returned to its place. After John, Ted said to Sarah,

"You'd better go first; "I watch from behind." Sarah went ahead and followed John, jumping up the stairs, and Ted went after Sarah.

John had almost reached the last stairs of the first row. The stairs were seven stations, each with seven steps, all of which were circular. The whole space was dark and the light was so bright that you could only see the next step. After each of the seven steps, there was a footstep for rest. John stood at the footstep of the door, and next to it was an hourglass, which began to move as soon as John reached there. And it was a sign of how long the foot-step would stay in place. A few seconds later, Sarah came to John, and at that moment, the hourglass moved faster.

"I don't think we can stand here long enough," John said. "We have to walk on this footstep just to rest before the end of the hourglass time." And then he jumped to the next step, and Sarah followed after a short pause. Ted was behind them, and as soon as Sarah left, the hourglass turned upside down. John told Ted aloud about the footstep and the hourglass so he could take a break.

John had reached the last foot-step, and there, he paused for a moment to rest. There were only seven steps left. John took a deep breath and prepared himself for the last steps. His leg muscles were a little tired and trembling as he jumped on the stairs. John counted the last steps: "One, two, three ..." On the third step, he paused for a moment and took a breath: "Four, five, six ..." When he jumped on the seventh step, the step from below John's legs disappeared and John plunged into darkness. John shouted; So Sarah and Ted heard John scream. "What happened?" Ted shouted from a distance.

"I do not know," said Sarah. "I think it was the sound of John screaming."

Sarah was in the footsteps of the last one and Ted before that. Sarah called out loudly to John but did not hear a sound. They were worried about John...

"I think something happened to John," Ted said. Be quick Sarah; we must hurry. Let me see what happened ..."

Sarah and Ted hurried to get to that point faster; unaware that John had fallen into darkness. Sarah had almost reached the last step; His legs were no longer strong; her muscles swelled from the intensity of the jumps and her heartbeat fast. She stood at the last step and put his hands on his knees and leaned forward. She took a breath. Meanwhile, Ted reached Sarah. Ted was very worried about John and did not think about his tiredness. When he reached Sarah, he said,

"Hurry up, Sarah!" It does not take long to stand here. "You go and then I will come."

"I'm out of breath," Sarah said. "If you can, go first so I can get some rest."

"Okay," Ted said. and moved to bring himself to John faster. Ted jumps the stairs very fast; like a gazelle roaming the mountains. Sarah also moved two steps behind Ted, so as not to fall far behind him. Ted reached the sixth step and took a breath, looking for John in the dark. After a short pause, when he saw no sign of John, he jumped to the seventh step, and the same thing happened to Ted, but Ted did not get a chance to shout; because he was shocked. His attention was on the other side of the stairs when he suddenly fell. Sarah, who was walking behind Ted, did not see Ted when she reached the sixth step, and she thought that he is on the other side was waiting for her and called Ted, but she did not hear anything. She got a little scared and jumped on the seventh step in fear, and then the same thing happened to Sarah.

John had been in the darkness for a long time; there seemed to be no end to this darkness. At the beginning of the fall, he was very scared; He thought that this is the end of the matter and everything is over and what a useless end...! Without achieving anything and without getting anywhere.

Everything was over. John thought of Ted and Sarah; To Professor and Ted's mother, who blamed him for Ted's trip. John prayed that Ted and Sarah, who had heard him shout, would not step on the seventh step. John was worried that they would suffer the same fate and fall into the well, but he did not know that they had not heard John's voice at all.

After a long time, John had experienced the fall at the same time, the fear of falling was gone, and he was more curious to know where this path would end; especially, that he did not see anywhere. From a distance, a light caught John's attention and it gradually approached the light source. He prepared himself for the end of the fall by hitting something. He was thinking about his unfulfilled dreams, when suddenly, in the last twenty meters, the situation changed. John was very slow; it is as if John is walking in space. He moved very slowly downwards until it was released at a distance of one meter, as if gravity had been reactivated, and collided with a soft, elastic object. After colliding with the object, a faint sound was heard and the object began to move. John tried to move, but he seemed to be nailed in place and unable to move. He felt heavy because of the free-fall he had. John felt he was riding an animal. He looked down. That moving object was green; with tiny purple spots. He looked forward; for a moment he saw a large head with large eyes looking at him and a voice coming out of the animal; it was as if the animal wanted to make John aware of something. After crossing an almost long road that reached the end of the path, the animal bent forward and pushed John with its tail. John slipped from behind the animal and fell into the waterfall from above his head, and fell with the waterfall as he screamed, and after going through the waterfall, he fell into the water and with the force that entered the water from below, he fell to the surface of the water. After reaching the water surface, he took a deep breath to feel better. At first, he started to stumble so as not to sink in the water, but after he got tired, he felt that he would not sink in the water at all and could easily lie on the water. John looked around; the color of the water was pink, and at the end of the part where the water was gathered, there was a river that was surrounded by trees in pink and blue. John decided to get out of the water and rest for a while, waiting to see if Ted and Sarah would follow him, and continue on their way together; so, he went to the beach and pulled himself out of the water. He stepped aside and threw himself on the grass that had grown by the river. And he breathed a sigh of relief that he had traveled this path in good health and reached this point. John was thinking to his friends where they are now! Did they have a problem? Maybe they heard John's voice and came back. It was in these thoughts that he heard the sound of something hitting the water and got up and looked at the water. Moments later, he saw Ted helping Sarah get on the water. He happily got up and ran to the water to help them and show himself to them and tell them where they were.

As soon as Sarah and Ted saw John, they called out and walked over to John. After seeing and embracing each other, John, Ted, and Sarah headed for the beach to rest and define this long journey. And think to continue the path. "We finally got you," Sarah said as they reached the beach. When you fell down the seventh floor, Ted and I heard you screaming and hurried after you. We thought something had happened to you or that a creature had attacked you. "I was very scared, and then when Ted moved in front of me and I was left alone, I followed the path you took."

"The important thing right now is that all three of us are safe and OK," John said.

"I was very worried," Ted said.

"The trees here are very interesting," Sarah said. "The color of the trees is blue and pink."

"The color of the water is also pink," Ted said. "Like chewing gum."

"There is a lake in Australia that looks like this pink water," Sarah said. The reason why the water there is pink is the creatures that live in the water, but I do not know here! Of course, I had not seen the color of the leaves of the trees; "It's like paradise here."

"It's as if, we died and came to heaven, and we do not know ourselves," Ted said.

"No, we will not die until this puzzle is solved," John smiled. "This path must end." And then he stared at the point that continued in the heart of the forest and along the river and thought...

Chapter Ten

Mysterious Forest

After resting and eating, they got ready to move: Ready to go into the mysterious forest and a new puzzle. John put his bag on his shoulders and said to Ted and Sarah, "Are you ready to go?"

They announced their readiness and all three went to the forest. At the entrance to the forest, they came across a strange corridor; Trees with no leaves were on either side of the entrance. There were only intricately twisted branches that came together on both sides and were intertwined; to create an impenetrable wooden roof. It was dark there too, and it was possible to walk with a stream of light shining through the branches. There, too, was a water stream that was moving upwards. Throughout that dark corridor, it was covered with branches, and the sound of a frog could be heard constantly. On both sides of the path and near the water stream, flowers with strange shapes had grown; the eyes of the animals could be seen in the dark, looking at them from a distance. "It's been very strange and a little scary," Sarah said as they walked some distance.

"Do not be afraid," Ted said. It's just a little dark here. I'm here."

"It's better to look at the map and see where we are on the path," John said. "And then he took the map out of his bag and spread it on the ground."

"It looks like we're on the right track, and the only way to get to that point is through this forest," Ted said. Look; there is no other path on the map. All the ways here are covered with trees; "This is the only way the map has shown."

"True, there is no other way," John said. OK; fortunately, we are on the right track. "We better keep going."

In the middle of the way, they felt that a creature was chasing them, and a sense of dread overtook them. They were constantly looking around. Suddenly a strange and frightening sound was heard from the heart of the forest, which sounded like a roar, and then, after a short pause, another sound was heard. It was as if someone begging for help in a language they did not understand, and then the earth began to shake and grow more and more; So that they could not maintain their balance.

"We'd better sit on the ground near that tree till the end of tremors," Ted said.

All three moved towards the tree. Extremely frightened, Sarah took Ted and John by the hand and closed her eyes.

The gap in the ground was not very deep or wide. The more they followed the gap, the wider the gap. It was clear that something had come out of the ground somewhere, and that the width of the gap was much wider. The ground had calmed down and those sounds had stopped. They took a deep breath as the sounds ran out.

"I do not think anything good is waiting for us," John said.

"You think the owner of that voice is so scary ..." Sarah said.

Sarah continued to speak in fear and could not finish.

"Don't worry," Ted said. Nothing happened to us. I believe." And he got up and, while shaking himself, continued: "We should continue on our way; "We wasted a lot of time."

"Do you think we should follow the path of the gaps?" "A feeling tells me that these gaps are leading us to where we want to be."

"I do not think so," said Sarah. "I think we are moving more towards that sound, and that is not good at all."

"It's better to follow the straight path and have nothing to do with these gaps at all, or maybe it's better to follow the path of this river," Ted said. I think it's better this way; "Isn't that so?"

"Okay," John said, "although I still believe the path is right to the center of the gaps, I have nothing to say." And then he got up and went to the river, and the others followed him without saying a word. They followed the path of the river; the farther they went, the less leafless the trees became, and the space above them became more open, and the light around them increased, and they were able to see their surroundings better. They had almost reached a point where there were no more leafless trees, and only occasionally saw willow trees and reached the plain. The river was gradually becoming a large river. After about two hours of walking, they reached the point where the river joined the lake. At the bottom of the river was a boat. It was as if they had left that boat for them.

"We'd better continue on this boat," Ted said. Without saying a word, John and Sarah got on the boat and boarded it. Ted did the same when he saw them. John and Ted went to the rowers and took the rowers.

"It's better to check the map before we go to make sure the path is right," Sarah said. After seeing the map, they found their position on the map and determined the continuation of the path, and continued on their way. Sarah used her compass to point the way. Sarah knew how to use a compass because of her job, and she could detect sea paths. John and Ted paddled, and Sarah marked the way for them. The humidity was very high; all three were drenched in sweat. Their water and food supplies were almost depleted. John and Ted stopped paddling to get some rest. Sarah got up and looked for something in the boat.

"What do you want, Sarah?" John said.

"I think there must be something to eat here," Sarah said.

"I do not think so," John said. I searched here well when I got on board; it was nothing."

Sarah sat on the bottom of the boat and, motionless, looked ahead.

"What do we do now?" Ted said. I can no longer paddle from hunger. I wish we were looking for food in the forest before boarding the boat; "Eventually something to eat was found."

John shrugged in desperation, folded his legs in his stomach, and placed his hands under his chin, and he, like Sarah, stared at the point and thought. Ted, who was starving and thirsty and could not just sit as the two of them, went to the water and put his feet in the water and a little later, jumped into the water. At the sound of Ted hitting the water, John and Sarah returned to the sound. Ted was swimming and shouting, "This is sweet water; "You can drink this water."

John and Sarah dipped their hands in water and eagerly drank all the water to be. This was good news; that at least one of their problems had been solved. After they had drunk enough water, John and Sarah jumped into the water and swam in the water like Ted until they regained their joy and their body temperature dropped. After swimming, they returned to the boat and lay on the bottom of the boat, looking up at the sky.

"Well," said Ted. The water problem is solved; what to do for food now? "Do you think there is anything to eat in the water?"

"If anything is found, I cannot eat it raw," John said.

"It's better than starving," Ted said.

While they were talking, part of the boat caught Sarah's attention. Sarah reached over and took a closer look. The bottom of the boat looked like a square, something like a hatch that has something like a handle. And right, there was a place where Ted was already sitting and rowing. "Please be quiet for a moment and come here ..." Sarah said loudly.

John and Ted looked at Sarah and got up and walked towards Sarah. Sarah showed them the hatch and said, "What do you think?"

"I do not think it's anything special," Ted said. Because this boat is small and cannot have a cabin under it. If you remember, this boat was on the shore and it was shallow there; remember that? "

"Yes," said John, "you are right; but why did they put such a thing on the boat?"Where did they want to go through this hatch?"

"Well, let's open it to see what it is," Ted said.

"I'm afraid that if we open it, it will be nothing and it will just push the water hard into the boat and we will drown," Sarah said.

"You're right," John said. "If that happens, we will not have a boat to go on."

"We do not have to open the entire hatch," Ted said. First, we open it very gradually; "If water does not enter the boat, then we will open it."

Sarah and John nodded in agreement. Ted went to the hatch and pulled the handle to himself, but to no avail; the hatch did not move.

"Let me help you," John said. And then they pulled the hatch handle together, but it still didn't work.

"I think this hatch has a key, or maybe it's not a hatch at all," said Ted.

"I do not think so," Sarah said. This hatch is neither useless nor has a key. "Can you go over there for me to try?"

Sarah approached the hatch, turned the lever down, and pulled the handle toward her. The hatch came up very slowly; she opened some of it, but there was no trace of water.

"You better open it completely," John said.

Sarah did the same; there were steps down the boat. Without hesitation, John stepped on the stairs and went downstairs, encountering an incredible scene. There was a room like a palace. There was a glass room and he could see under the sea. Something like a complete house ... there were three beds; Bathroom, toilet, kitchen, gas, boiler, and a refrigerator full of food...! »

"This is unbelievable," John said. "What's unbelievable?" Said Sarah and Ted from the top of the boat.

"You better come down and see by yourself," John said.

Ted and Sarah went downstairs and were shocked to see that luxurious room under the boat; Of course, they were happy that there was such a thing under the boat.

"But ... how is that possible?" Ted said. "Something like this under this boat and somewhere near the shore!"

"Just as we saw other impossible things in the way and it became possible," Sarah said.

Ted smiled and said, "Yeah, you're right.”I forgot that this is different from the real world." And then he went to the refrigerator, and he was happy to see the food, and he took some of it and gave it to John and Sarah, and he said, 'We have food here for a month. It was great; "At least, we know we are not starving." Then he took a big bite of the chicken sandwich in his hand, filled his lips, and continued with his mouth full: "This is great! It gives an extraordinary taste; "I have not eaten such food for a long time." and continued to eat more quickly.

When they got tired of eating, they just remembered the curiosity in that cabin.

"It's really beautiful here ... an underwater glass room," John said.

"Yeah," Ted said, "it's like we're in an aquarium and the fish are looking at us from the outside."

Sarah went to the front of the cabin and carefully inspected it; there was a helm; it was also a TV-like screen that showed the top of the boat and its front. Sarah looked at the screen in front of her; there was a button, and Sarah pressed it. The boat started to move and slowly moved the lever next to the button; the speed of the boat increased, but inside the cabin, they did not feel any movement. There was a large compass on the screen that showed them the direction of movement.

"I wish we had found this place from the beginning so we wouldn't paddle so much," Ted said. But now it is very good; the speed of the boat was not high. "It was not more than ten kilometers per hour."

Sarah was riding the boat, and John and Ted were sitting next to her. Ted looked at the screen and John saw the fish passing by behind the glass. Ted saw a picture of a cave on the boat screen and said to Sarah, "What do you think of that?"

"I think, it is a cave," Sarah said.

John was fascinated by Sarah and Ted.

"I think we have to go through that cave," Sarah said.

John looked at the map and said, "Yes, there is no other way."We have to get through here."

Sarah steered the boat toward the cave. When they reached the entrance of the cave, the boat stopped moving; it was as if its engine had stopped.

Ted turned to John and said, "I think we should paddle the rest of the way again; "Let's go up."

The three returned to the surface of the boat. Sarah sat on the tip of the boat. At the beginning of the entrance to the cave, its height was very low; so the bottom of the boat had to be stretched to pass through its mouth; they could hardly get through it and enter the cave.

Chapter Eleven

Entering the Castle

When they entered the cave, they were amazed by the pictures on the cave wall as well as the shapes created by the water sediment. The paintings on the cave walls were carved that look old, the image of the hunting of a huge animal, the animal of which was not known, by three men. Picture of a woman lighting a fire and cooking; Other images that show the way of life in ancient times; Also, due to the deposition of water, shapes such as a double dragon, the head of an elephant, and various other things were created. Sarah, who was as interested in these things as her father, was attracted to these images and looked at them with interest. Then she said to himself, "I wish my father was here!"

As they watched the pictures, the stream of water moved the boat forward. As they approached the bottom of the cave, John suggested they return to the cabin. They had almost reached the bottom of the cave when suddenly a hatch opened in a part of the land inside the cave and the boat fell. The boat was moving on something like a water slide. As soon as it fell, all three cried out unconsciously. The boat slammed into the water and moved forward with great speed. A few minutes later, at the end of the slippery slope, the boat soared into the air, then plunged into the water in a free fall and went straight into the water, calming down without any damage. Ted, John, and Sarah, nauseous from the ups and downs, splashed water on their faces to make them feel better.

"I think we should go the rest of the way underwater," Sarah said.

"Let's take a look at the map," John said. And spread the map on the bottom of the boat. The point where they were was marked on the map; Right in front of them was a huge mountain under which water flowed. They had to cross the mountain in the same boat as a submarine.

"Very well," Ted said. So let's move on. "Time should not be wasted."

Sarah went to the helm and pressed the engine start button, moved the lever, and moved the boat, which had now become a submarine.

There was a small hole in the mountain that two or three boats could pass through. Sarah steered the boat in that direction and slowly entered the crevice of the mountain through a narrow mouth; nothing could be seen and it was absolute darkness. The boat lights were on automatically and only light could be seen pointing in the opposite direction to avoid hitting anything. After crossing that gap, the boat landed on a belt at the end of the gap, and the cabin under them moved upwards. "The roof over their heads rose and fell on the boat, and there was no more news of the cabin."

The boat was out of the water and was going up with a conveyor belt. They just watched what was happening around them and saw how it was about to happen. After some distance up, the boat moved towards the platform and got out of the belt. They took their belongings from the boat and went to the platform. When they got off, a hatch opened under the boat, and the boat went down, disappearing.

In front of them was an exit similar to the entrance to a cave, and seemed the only way out. "We'd better go this way," John said. And all three went in the same direction as John said. After a short walk, a light was seen in the distance.

"I think we finally got out of the cave and out of the mountain," Sarah said.

That cave was the way out of that mountain and they came out of the cave. The other side of the cave was covered with beautiful trees. The beach was golden sand and shone in the sun; the beach was covered with oysters in beautiful colors.

"Kids ... look over there," Ted said. And then he pointed to the island that was beyond their island. Conical islands are suspended between the earth and the sky and covered with trees. On the other side of them, several small islands hung in the air, around the larger island. Inside the island were monkey-like animals with outstretched arms and large, black eyes and small heads that jumped up and down trees like monkeys and walked from island to island.

"I think we died and entered heaven," Sarah said. "It's very beautiful here."

"I do not think so," Ted said. "If it was heaven, I would not be here now." And he smiled and said, "Oh, my father always said, you are in hell."

"It's really beautiful here," John said. "I do not want to leave here and I would like to be here for the rest of my life."

"Did you guys notice the beach sand here?" Ted said. "Do you think this is gold?"

"It's better to pack some of these and try them out later," Sarah said.

John punched some of the sand to put it in his bag, but when he tried to pour a handful of dirt into the bag, he had nothing in his hand. He tried several times, but each series was empty-handed. "It's no use," John said. "It's as if we are not allowed to take them away."

"We'd better go into the woods and find a place to rest," Ted said. "I am tired of this voyage."

They entered the forest to find a resting place. The color of the trees and flowers there was very beautiful; the sound of birdsong and the sound of a waterfall could be heard from afar.

"Do you hear the sound of water?" Said, John.

"Yeah, we'd better go to the soundtrack and rest there," Sarah said.

Ted, John, and Sarah made their way through the rocky path and through the trees and foliage that covered it everywhere, to the sound of the water until they reached a height and encountered a beautiful waterfall. And the waterfall led to the river. John went to the river and splashed some water on his face. Ted put his head close to the water and drank the water, and Sarah went to the waterfall and put her hand under the water.

When John saw his picture in the water, he looked like his father. John dipped his hand in the water and shattered the image on the water. He looked at the waterfall and saw the picture of the same man again and heard the man laughing. "I saw the picture of the same man I first saw in that spring,"

John told Ted. Here it was in that waterfall; "He wants to tell us something." And the picture began to speak:

"You finally got here; Congratulations John! As I thought you were an intelligent boy and you were able to get yourself to this point. There is a volcano behind this forest that after passing that volcano, you can reach the castle. Prepare yourself for new events. "I see you in the castle." And the image disappeared from the waterfall.

"It's like this trip is not over," John said.

"It's better to look for food first and then find a place to sleep," Ted said. "Because we have a difficult journey ahead."

Feeling tired, Sarah found a soft spot in a corner of the space under a tree and fell asleep. Ted and John also started a fire. Unlike other places, the plain they reached had a sky, the air was dark and the stars were visible in the sky. Ted and John sat around the fire. Ted was drawing shapes on the ground with a stick in his hand, and John was looking at the sky. Ted stopped drawing the line on the ground and turned to John, saying, "John, you know something ... Ever since you left the orphanage and had no place to live, there has never been a chance or Maybe I was scared or embarrassed to ask you how you lived! "How are you doing?"

"Those days were the worst time of my life," John said. I would look for food in the dumpster and sleep at night under the stairs or in the sleeping quarters of the homeless. In the winter I shivered from the cold until one night when I was tired of life, I was talking to God in a secluded place about why all the bad things should happen to me! Why all the misery just for me! Do you exist at all? Maybe he is not a God at all. "Maybe in this world, everything is lucky, and there is no God at all ... It was after that when I found that dumpster, and then I understood the story of my parents and came to the conclusion that nothing is lucky."

"I disagree with you," Ted said. I believe that everything in this world is based on luck; because finding that dumpster was also a chance. You just got in the right place at the time and had a chance to find that. "If you had not been there, you would not be here now and it was not clear what would have happened to you, or my friend, who was born into a rich family, could have lived like this if he were in a poor family."

"I do not deny luck at all," John said. In some things, luck is involved, but not everything goes by chance, and it is not like sitting on one side and waiting for a chance to hit your door. "Look, Ted, many scientists or artists, and great people were not born into a wealthy family, but were able to find their way." And then he turned to the sky and pointed to a star with his hand and continued: "Do you see that big star? If we consider that big star as luck, there is a smaller star in that star and there are points of light in that smaller star; some flashing light. This is our big star of luck; the smaller star can be our environment, family, and friends, and the small point that is blinking is me, with my efforts and choices, can illuminate that star. If I had not tried to continue my life or chosen the right path, this star would have disappeared now. Everyone's star is indeed different, but there are similarities. I looked at the lives of successful people and found similarities between my star and theirs and came to the conclusion that I could be like them; When I was walking the streets and I could not walk due to extreme hunger, I came across many people who were financially great in the past, but they got to that point by making the wrong choice. If you had continued with your old friends, now instead of being with me, you might have gone a very bad way. God has given us the right to choose, but He always wants the best for us. If we choose correctly, we will reach the peaks. Sometimes, there is a very easy way to succeed and reach higher levels, but since we think that to reach higher places, we have to go through a difficult and tortuous path, we do not think so. Let this be the right path. There is a loser in life that is not even willing to try for fear of failure. "I overcame this fear and I am sure that God is always with someone who is on the right path."

"Characteristically, life on the street has made you very mature," Ted said. The words you say are the words of philosophers; my brain does not pay much attention to these things, but since I know you are the right child, I accept the nonsense. "Let's sleep now because we have a long way to go tomorrow."

John got up laughing at Ted and looked for a soft place to sleep. Ted, like John, found a soft spot and they slept peacefully.

When they woke up in the morning, they ate a small breakfast and got ready to leave...

Crossing the forest, they reached the castle. A castle with seven floors; seven towers of the same size ... They went to the castle but found no door.

"There are no doors here, either hidden in the castle or the entrance is from somewhere else," John said.

Sarah, turning her head this way and that to perhaps find a door, noticed the high hedges a little further from the castle.

Sarah pointed to the hedges and said, "Look there; I think we should go that way; "Maybe we will find something."

John and Ted followed Sarah without question, and there was a wooden room just behind the hedges. Sarah opened the door and entered the room. Despite the daylight, it was completely dark inside the room. Sarah subconsciously looked for a key to turn on the light and found a key and pressed it, but by pressing that key, she emptied under her feet and was led down a slide that was down. John and Ted, who had heard Sarah's voice when she fell, entered the room and they repeated the same thing and the same thing happened to them. Minutes later, John and Ted joined Sarah. All three had entered the castle; the entrance to the castle had a high ceiling, and the paintings on the roof were a combination of forest and sky.

No one was waiting for them in that castle. In front of them was a corridor that reached the stairs at the end and was the entrance to the castle floors.

"I don't think we should procrastinate anymore," Ted said. "We have to go up the stairs and discover the world of this castle."

After 77 steps, they reached the first floor and entered. First Ted came in and then Sarah and the last person who came in was John. Room floor with black and white square stones; Like a chessboard, it was paved and had a brown border around the chessboard. The walls were full of blank paintings. There were no windows or lights, but the room was bright.

Ted was looking at the blank boards, moving from the side of the chessboard. The only painting inside one of those empty frames caught Ted's attention and he moved toward the painting to see it. After a few moments, Sarah saw the picture and walked towards the painting like Ted; suddenly the roof opened and the double-edged ax moved toward Ted. Seeing the scene, John shouted, "Watch out, Ted."

Ted was frozen in fear and could not move, and the double-edged ax reached Ted and he turned back. The next moment, from where Sarah was standing, bars fell from the ceiling, and the six bars fell exactly on the sides of the square where Sarah was standing. Sarah screamed in fear. It was not long before John shouted: "Be quiet! "Nothing has happened." Sarah calmed down a bit and wanted to move, but John shouted again, "Do not move." And Sarah stood up at John's command. John looked carefully at the surfaces on which Ted and Sarah were standing. They were both standing on black houses.

"I think something would happen if we stood on the black houses," John said. "It is better not to step on black houses at all."

"So what do we do?" Said Ted, who had just recovered from the shock of previous events. It's better to look for a way out of this room. "I do not see the exit door here."

"I think there's something in this frame that has to do with getting out of here," Sarah said.

"Look, can you see something?" John said to Ted, who was in front of Sarah.

"It's as if a text, like a poem, was written here," Ted said.

"Can you read?" John said.

Ted paid a little attention and read the poem:

"Seven bodies, seven ways of searching;

Seven houses, Go ahead because behind it;

The other way is to be obvious;

See the sentences now, so you read ..."

"I can read this far," Ted said. The frame is very high and the rest of the writing is very small; "It cannot be seen."

"What does it mean by seven bodies?" Sarah said.

Whatever John thought, nothing came to his mind.

"Look at the walls," Ted said. There is a column on each wall; "Do you think there is anything inside the columns?"

"Let me see," John said.

John reached the first column from the right, around the edge of the chessboard, tapped on the wall, touched a key, and pressed it. From inside the ground, the king's piece in the White House came out of the first row in the middle houses. He reached to the second column and repeated it, and the minister's piece came out in the White House, one-piece ahead of the king; in the same way, the other pieces came out by moving and pushing John's hand on the wall. The pawn was the last piece that comes out from the one before the last square.

"John, I think we have to move on the pieces so we can get to the end," Ted said.

John did the same and jumped over the pieces to get to the pawn, but nothing was known from there.

"I think you have to do the pawn's last move," Sarah said.

Without any further thought, John jumped from the top of the pawn piece to the white house facing him, and as soon as he jumped on the white screen, he went down and John fell to the ground and after a moment he was thrown up from another house. It came out of the ground and John fell on the stairs. He climbed the stairs so that he could read the rest of the poem on the frame. It was written in small letters: "Always move up."

John looked over his head and tried to push the ceiling. The door opened with a push on the ceiling. "The way out has been found," John shouted happily.

Sarah and Ted, like John, moved on the pieces, climbed the stairs, and left the room. They climbed 77 steps again, but there was no door. It was just a resting place to freshen up a bit. There seemed to be a door to enter only in the odd floors; so they went up another 77 steps and reached the third floor, pressing the door and entering. Like the first floor, it disappeared after the entrance was closed.

A small light shone from the ceiling to the floor, and the wall of the room was circular. The walls were cut in half, with half moving clockwise and the other half counterclockwise. Sarah was looking for a way out. The light shining from the ceiling caught her attention. She moved towards it so that she might find a way out.

There were constellations on the roof of that room, as well as planets moving in the same order in space, and that light was like the sun. Sarah moved towards the light and sat down under it and looked at the light. Sarah stared at the light and no longer blinked; it was as if she was no longer in that world. The planets moving on the roof were all in a parallel line. After a few seconds, the walls remained fixed, creating an image like a movie screen.

Sarah was still facing the light and her eyes were wide open. The pictures on the wall began to move; it was pictures of Sarah as a child reading a book with a younger professor.

The next picture was inside the professor's library; Sarah was a teenage girl who seemed to be hiding in a corner of the library, and the professor was talking to a man who was talking about a book on an important topic. Sarah's body, which was still in place, began to shake. That memory is not a good one. At that moment, Ted decided to shake Sarah to free her from the situation and destroy the light relationship with Sarah, so he quickly moved towards Sarah and knocked her to the ground. Ted fell heavily on Sarah. As they fell, Sarah screamed and shouted, "What are you doing, Ted?"

Ted hurriedly got up from Sarah and held out his hand to Sarah. Sarah, seemingly unaware of herself, shook Ted's hand, got up, and shook herself angrily. Ted, who was upset with Sarah, became angry and, not knowing what to say, went to the wall and punched the wall.

The planets on the roof began to move after Sarah and Ted fell to the ground; just like the previous stage, the walls started to move. John went to Sarah and explained the matter to her. "I forgot a lot of these memories myself," Sarah said in surprise. It's very interesting! "How these memories came to my mind!"

"How do you think this story is going to help us get out of here?" John said. "Then turned to: Ted, you have no idea?"

Ted, still angry with Sarah, shook his head. Sarah, who had just understood the matter, went to Ted and took his hand and squeezed him and apologized to Ted. Ted smiled and accepted Sarah's apology. Ted said with the same smile to John: "I think you should stand under that light like Sarah."I think there is something in your mind that can help you get out of here."

"I think you're right; "So I would better do the same." And then he moved on to the light and continued, "Whatever happened, you better not do the same to me like what you did to Sarah."

When John stood in Sarah's previous position, a light struck John from behind and came out of his forehead, shining into the center of the moving walls, and the walls stopped moving and a picture was painted on the wall; It was a picture of John, but it was a place where it was not clear. It was like a desert. John was in that picture at the same age, and he was stunned by where he was. It seemed that John's body was in the room, but his soul was somewhere else. John runs around in the desert, but gets nowhere and finds nothing. Ted called out loud to John, but it was as if you could not hear him. "Ted wanted to do what he did with Sarah to cut off the light, but Sarah stopped him, saying it was John's decision and insisting that we do nothing unless there was a danger to John." We have to see what happens; "The way out of the room must be determined."

Meanwhile, John, who was in the picture, stopped moving and suddenly turned around and asked, "Where is the way out?"

Hypnotized, John inadvertently raised his hand and pointed to the wall in front of him, and John said in the picture, "But there's nothing!"

John raised his hand again and pointed to the same point, and John in the picture went to the other side and walked away from the picture and left and nothing could be seen but the desert.

Ted walked over to John and shook him. With Ted shaking, John fell to the ground, out of hypnosis, and immediately asked, "What happened?" Were you able to understand something? "Did you see anything?"

Ted told him the story of John's picture in the desert, and John, after hearing Ted talk, said, "Why are you waiting? This is a sign. We have to search that wall. Surprised, Sarah turned around and said, "You mean you weren't surprised by this story at all?"

"Of course," John said. But now there is something more important than that. I do not have time to think about other things. "The important thing now is that he told us the way out."

"Of course, it was your twin brother who almost showed the way," Ted said.

Ignoring Ted's words, John got up, went to the wall, and began to search for a sign to leave the room. Ted and Sarah joined John. They were searching when John's foot slipped on a piece of rock next to the wall, and the stone went down, and the opposite wall moved slightly forward, but could not pass over it. John stepped forward and pushed the wall, but the wall did not move. And then he looked for something else to move the wall again. What he was looking for was, in fact, the next rock on earth. John stepped on it, and again the wall went back one stone-sized, and space was opened for them to leave. It was completely dark on the other side of the door, but as soon as they stepped into it, it lit up and they could see the stairs. So they immediately went to the fifth floor and went up the 77 steps again, and after some rest, they went up the second 77 steps and reached the fifth floor, and entered the room.

The fifth-floor room was the glass; As if suspended between earth and sky; There was no wall, no ceiling, not even the floor. When they looked down, they saw the earth from a great distance. They looked up, they saw the sky, and there was no wall. After seeing this scene, all three were dizzy with fear and fell on the ground whose surface was invisible.

John tried to move forward crawling. After moving forward a little, his head hit the object firmly. John rubbed his head to ease the pain. He reached out to touch the object his head had hit and realized that his head had hit a wall that was not as visible as the floor and ceiling of the room but was there. The challenge of this room was to find a door that was on a wall and was invisible. After touching the wall, John overcame his fear and stood on his feet, and began to touch the wall. Ted and Sarah still could not stand on their feet for fear. John caught their attention by calling Sarah and Ted.

"Get up," John said. This room, like other rooms, has doors, walls, ceilings, and floors; "It's just invisible and we have to find the exit."

Ted and Sarah heard John's words, they put aside their fears, and slowly reached for John, who was touching the wall, to help John find the exit door; But the further they went, the less they came to conclusion, and the closer they got to despair.

They were tired; almost they searched every wall from top to bottom several times, but there was no sign of the entrance or exit door. Tired of this, they sat on the ground. John leaned his head against the wall, hugged his knees, and meditated. Meanwhile, a cool breeze caressed John's face.

"This is the wall, but I do not know where this breeze is coming from," John said.

"It must have a window that is not visible," Ted said.

As Ted said this, Sarah blinked and said, "This is the way out ... this could be a sign; "It means a place from here that can be got out of there."

"Oh, we've got everywhere," Ted said.

"Not everywhere," John said. We just looked at the walls. "We did not search the roof and the floor." And after that sentence, he started walking on the floor of the room. Sarah and Ted were searching, but again to no avail. They met at one point and then looked at each other all three of them were laying on the ground at the same time and all three of them were staring at the sky and thinking about how to search the roof? "Meanwhile, a breeze caressed the faces of all three again."

Ted said, "John, you better get on my shoulder and reach out; "Maybe you can touch somewhere."

John and Ted, without question, got up and did what Ted had said, but to no avail. No matter how hard John tried and reached out, his hand would not get anywhere; it was as if it had no roof at all, or if it did, it was too high and their hands could not reach the ceiling.

Disappointed again, they sat down and thought.

Sarah said: kids, you know! Here is like the human mind. Both closed and open; It is closed in the material world and is beyond anything in the other world. The human brain is inside a room called the skull, but it cannot limit it, and just to protect it, the human mind can go beyond the earth and discover planets and much more. I have always seen people with their minds bending a spoon or stopping something. The question for me was how high the power of the mind is and how effective it can be for us. John, for example, your age is not very old, but with the power of your mind and the desires you had, you were able to reach the point where you are now, where many others could not reach this point; "Because they did not want to get here from the bottom of their hearts."

"That's right," John said. But unfortunately, many people misuse this power and go to dangerous places, destroying themselves and humanity; "I wish human beings were not allowed to misuse such powers!"

"At that time, human free will had no meaning and the meaning of good and bad was not clear," Sarah said. "As long as it is not bad, good does not make sense."

A breeze blew on their faces again; "I think it's the brain's assurance valve that when it heats up like my brain, it blows air so that it doesn't explode," Ted said. And all three laughed.

"Sarah, now that you've talked about the power of the mind and said you can go to the galaxy and elsewhere with your mind, come and try it and try to get out of here with your mind," Ted said.

"I do not think I have that much power," Sarah said. "I mean, I have not tried yet."

"There is no harm in trying it," John said.

"I've read a lot of books on the subject, but I've not tried it yet," Sarah said.

"An inactive man, like a bee without honey," Ted said. If you just sit down every day and read a book and say excellent, nothing in your life will happen. You have to believe in what you read and believe in what you do. If this is not the case, reading a thousand books is useless; you just wasted your life. I do not read books myself; I mean, I love it, but since I know I'm stubborn and I do not act on the book I read, and that book has a good-bad effect on me, and then, I'm all trying to make excuses, but you're not like that. ; At least for the last few times, I have not seen you like this. You are a pragmatist; now is the time to act on the books you have read; At least you can tell if what is said in the books is true or not. "That way, at least the task becomes clear to you, and you have no idea what it would be like if I did that."

Confused and knowing that Ted's words were right, Sarah shrugged and said, "Well, his efforts are not in vain; "In your opinion, at least it turns out how true the book's words are, but that book did not say you could go anywhere."

"You do not need to move from one place to another," John said. "This is not our job and it requires a lot of practice, but at least you can concentrate and ask your conscience to find a way out of here."

Sarah sat down on the floor. She closed her eyes and put her hands on his feet, imagining in her mind the way out of the room and asking her conscience to show her a way out. A few minutes passed, but there was no news. Sarah got tired and opened her eyes and said, "No; I cannot; "Because I have not practiced this before."

"You have to," Ted said. I'm sure you can. I see that there is high power and positive energy in you; "You better try again."

Without a question, Sarah closed her eyes again, took a deep breath, and regained the previous mood. Suddenly Sarah felt the need to look down. She did not know why this thought came to her mind! She was also in the middle of thinking about the way out. She tried to get rid of what she thought was a disturbing thought, but no matter how hard she tried, the thought of looking at the floor of the room, which was originally an image of the floor, did not leave her mind; That's why she opened her eyes.

"Could you understand something?" John said.

"No," Sarah said, "but I always have a disturbing thought."

"What thought?" Said Ted.

"When I want to focus on the way out of here, I always think about looking at the ground from here," Sarah said.

"Maybe that's the idea of leaving," John said. "Maybe something came to your mind."

"Isn't it the case that whatever you want in your mind, it gives it to you or shows you the way," Ted said. The mind that is not human, come and tell you to come this way out. Something inspires you that is a sign. To get it right, everything that inspires you must have a reason or you wanted to get it; now it can be good or bad. "The important thing is that you wanted it."

"Yeah, right," Sarah said. I always thought I should see something strange now; it is better to act on the idea of looking at the ground; "Maybe we found something."

Sarah looked at the ground and looked for a sign on the ground. As she walked and looked at the ground, she saw trees that, together, formed the word "love".

"Kids, look at the trees that made the word love together," Sarah said.

John and Ted, no matter how careful they were, did not see such a thing. Whatever Sarah was pointing at, they could not see. Sarah got up to show them the place of the words and said, "Pay attention to my footsteps, the words are exactly where I walk." And then, without hesitation, she got up and started walking on the word love to show its place to John and Ted.

When Sarah showed the last word and stepped aside, all three of them suddenly heard a sound and subconsciously turned to the sound and noticed that a square piece had protruded from the wall in front of them and a picture of one hand was on it.

"I think this is the way out," Ted said. And he went to the part of the wall where the brick had come out. When he reached that point, he pressed the brick, but to no avail.

"Maybe you'd better put your hand in place of the hand," Sarah said.

Ted did the same, but it was much more delicate than Ted's hand, and Ted's hand did not fit there.

"I think this is your hand placement," Ted told Sarah. My hand does not fit here; "You better try."

Sarah got up and went to the wall and put her hand on it; the place of the hand on the brick was exactly the size of Sarah's hand. "It was as if it had been cut off for her hand."

Everyone was waiting for something to happen by putting Sarah's hand on the brick, but nothing happened; all three were disappointed and at the same time sat on the ground and leaned against the wall.

"Maybe there was no way out," John said.

"But I'm sure there's a way out," Ted said. "Otherwise, it would not have occurred to Sarah to go downstairs." And then he turned to Sarah and continued, "But I still do not see that word."

"It's weird for me," Sarah said. And she pointed to the word love again and said, "There it is; "Right there."

Ted noticed and instead of the word love, he saw the word honesty and shouted, "I saw ... I saw."

"Thank God," Sarah said. "Finally you saw it."

"I saw," Ted said. But it is the word honesty. "I did not see the word love."

"But I do not see such a word there," said Sarah.

"I think everyone only sees one word," John said. "I think you should do Sarah's job," he told Ted.

"What should I do?"Said Ted.

"Walk on the word of honesty," John said.

Ted got up and did the same thing, knocking out another brick on the wall with a hand carving that was about the size of Ted's hand.

"Now it's your turn, John, to see your word," said Sarah. "I do not think anything can be done with two bricks."

John stared down at the ground and a few minutes later saw the word courage. He also showed the word of courage by walking on it and the next brick came out of the wall.

"Now I realize that these words are the hallmarks of each of us," Sarah said. "At John, courage is the highest attribute that has been able to overcome many difficulties alone and get here, and in Ted, as expected, honesty is paramount."

"Like most women, love is more evident in you than anything else," said Ted, blushing at the definition.

Sarah laughed and said, "We'd better go and put our hands on the bricks to see what happens." And the three of them went to the wall and put their hands in a certain place. After all three touched the bricks, the glass room disappeared and all three were on the stairs.

"We came out of this room safe," John said.

"I want to call this room the Mind Room," Ted said. "Because, as Sarah puts it, this room is like a mind."

"Yeah, I think it's a good name," Sarah said.

"Then go to the last room," John said. And all three of them went up the stairs.

They had reached the seventh floor. On the seventh floor was a tall gold-colored door. On either side of them were statues of lion heads screaming. The large door was seemingly heavy; "Three of us should help each other and push the door open," Ted said.

They opened the door and all three entered. The room was large and luxurious with a high ceiling. There were various paintings on the ceiling. There were six pictures on the walls; three photos on the left and three photos on the right. There was a blank photo frame on the wall in front of the front door. The room was large and new; Gold furniture was arranged in it. All three were amazed watching the beauty there and for a moment forgot where they were. They heard a voice that greeted them, and all three returned to the voice. Someone was standing in the corner of the room with his face in the shadows and could not be seen.

"Finally you were able to get here," the voice said. John said to the voice, "Yes, we have finally arrived."

The man came forward and his face appeared; He was the same person they had seen before and at the beginning of the journey. "I endured all this hardship to ask you the answers to the questions that are on my mind," John said.

"Ask," said Mr. Bellini.

"Who am I and why did you drag me here?" John said.

"It's better to answer your questions yourself than another person," said Andreas Bellini.

There was a sound of the door opening, it was not clear where it came from, and then the sound of his footsteps approached them.

"Very welcome, little John," the man said. I would love to see you up close. "Andreas praised you a lot."

The voice got closer and closer to them, and the person's face became more visible. That person was quite similar to John but older. All three looked completely surprised and with open mouths. "I'm John Wilson," the man said.

John could not speak in surprise and only looked at the great John Wilson.

"I know you were very surprised how much I looked like little John," said John Wilson the Great. Welcome to our world. Here is a world parallel to your world. "I'm John Wilson, but 700 years older than little John."

"It's not possible," Sarah said. "You mean you are 700 years old?"

"Yes, time in our world is different from yours, and our life in this world is clear," John the Great said. We already know when we will die. Everyone lives here for 700 years. "We have seven periods of life here, every period is a hundred years and then we close our eyes and die."

"How are you and me similar?" John said. "Even though we are 700 years apart in age!"

John the great said, "I will be twins with one of your ancestors, whose name was also John and like me, and you are the last person from the generation that is in the last year of my life."When we are born, a person is born with us in your world, and in the last period of our lives, another person from the same generation as the first and seventh person, who is my name and like us."

"So what if someone in our world does not get married or get married but has no children?"

"That person only lives to be a hundred years old and then dies," said John the Great.

"So you mean someone is like me in this world right now?" Sarah said.

"Yes," said John the Great, "but it is not clear how old he is now." "It is not clear which generation of your people you are!"

Little John said, "Is there any other world than this?"

"Yes," said John the Great, "there are seven worlds in parallel, and your world and ours are two of these seven worlds."

"Have you seen other worlds?" John asked.

John the Great replied, "No, they are very far from here, and I have not yet been able to go to those worlds, but according to the writings which have long been given to us and told to us. ¬We know how the world is drawn and what other worlds exist, but nothing is said about their details. "I was able to find your world with a lot of searching."

"Do other people in your world all live in this castle?" Ted said.

"No, our cities are out of here and the people of this world are somewhere else," John the Great said. "Everyone in this world has a palace like this for himself/herself, in which all his/her relatives and people live."

Little John asked, "Then why did I not see anyone here?"

"Because I have no wife and no children," said John the Great.

"Mr. Bellini?" John said.

"Mr. Bellini came from your world," said John the Great.

"Then someone else came to this world before us," said little John.

"Several years ago, when I discovered your world, I was on my way to your world when I met Andreas and talked to him about my world," said John the Great. Andreas talked to his trusted friends about it, and they came into my world to get gold, but they did not tell me anything, and I accepted. They took my gold without informing me and Andreas, and one day secretly escaped from here, but they did not know that in this world if something is taken without permission, it will cause severe calamities and problems. The skeleton you saw in front of the entrance is the skeletons of the same people who were each killed for a reason. "Andreas, who came with them, wanted to stay with me for the rest of his life."

"So you mean Andreas is old now?" Sarah said.

"Yes," said the John the Great, "whoever lives in this world, even if he/she is born in another world, lives seven hundred years according to the laws of our world."

"In this world, where do you get your tools?" Ted said. "I mean, is there a mall or a factory?"

"We do not need to invent anything," said John the Great. It will be provided whenever we want or whatever we want."

"It's great," Ted said, and immediately asked for a hamburger, and the hamburger came to the table.

"Wow," Ted said. This is great! "I no longer need to work here, and I can eat whatever I want."

"Why did you want me to get here?" Said little John.

"In our world, if you have no children or relatives after you, all that you have will be destroyed," John the Great said. "I do not have anyone, I wanted in my world, the person who is my last twin, to own my property."

"So why did you communicate with my father before through Andreas," John said.

"I wanted your parents to come here with you, but unfortunately that event happened," John the Great said. "Your father was smart, but not as clever as you are."

"Then why did you put all those problems in my way?" John said.

"To make sure that the one who replaces me can endure all this hardship," said John the Great.

"This is great, John," Ted said. "We can live here easily."

"That's great," said Sarah, looking happy.

"You both have families," John said. "You mean you do not want to go back to them?"

She turned to John the Great and said, "Can we bring them with us?"

"John must ask," said John the Great. "It's up to John and he can decide."

"But I do not want to live here," John said.

Ted and Sarah smiled and both of them said, "Why?"

"Life is meaningless here," John said. You live in a place where you make no effort to achieve your desires and pursue a life without purpose. In my opinion, if a person is supposed to live even one year, he/she should have a goal for that one year as well. When you know the time of your death, that life has no excitement for you. When everything you want is provided to you, no more ideas come to your mind and the creativity of your mind disappears. This world is like a prison. A life for which you have no policy is not interesting to me. My purpose in coming here was not to make money; I was more curious to know what my father was looking for and for what he lost his life. I like to enjoy life, with all its unforeseen events. "That everything is ready for you is beautiful at first, but then it repeats itself."

"But I love living this way," Sarah said. "It's a pity we can't be here until you let and come here."

"John may not be here, but let you be here, and he can come here," said John the Great.

If you do, Andreas can stay here too; "Otherwise, he will have to return to your world and die sometime later."

"I have no problem with anyone staying here, and maybe I'll come here again," John said.

"I want to be with John always," Ted said.

"So we'd better go back to our world and bring my grandfather with me," Sarah said. "I'm sure he likes it."

John the Great said, "You can like me, who sought other worlds and found your world, seek other worlds."Given the documents I have and the signs I have, you can look for signs."

John, who had not yet found what he was looking for, lost all his excitement, and when he heard the great John's offer, he became excited again and blinked his eyes, saying, "This offer is great and it can eliminate the useless of living here; "This is something that can be achieved in this world."

"Something has been written about the existence of parallel universes in our science books and other books, but so far no one has been able to prove it," Sarah said.

The great John said, "Surely those worlds exist; "Like our world and yours."

"By the way, are you staying here, too?" Ted said.

"Yes, I will stay," John said. But first, I have to go back to our world and I have some small things to do and then I go back. "If you want to bring someone with you, you have to come back."

John turned to John the Great and said, "Do we have to go the same hard way to get back from here?"

"No, there is no need," said John the Great. You can go back to the fifth floor, the room you named the room of the mind. "Andreas will come with you and tell you how to return to your world and how to come here again."

"Great," said John. So let's go. "The professor has thought until now that we are dead."

"In your world, the seven days you have been down here, seven hours have passed," said John the Great.

You have to keep in mind that when you return to your world, you have the opportunity to stay there for seven days, and you must return to this world at the end of the seventh day. "I will die after these seven days, and you will ascend to the throne of this palace."

"These seven days are just because of your death?" John said.

"No, it is always like that," said John the Great. "The time to be away from this world is only seven days, and you cannot be further away from here."

"I wish we had postponed your death," John said. "I just found you and I can learn a lot from you."

John the Great said, "I have left many writings for you; "By reading them, you can find a way to live here. Andreas and my servants are also here and can help you."

"When we bring our family, do we have to live in the same rooms we went through?" Ted said.

"I wanted the floors to be like that," John the Great said. You can live on even floors. On those floors, we can create as many rooms as you want; "Rooms that have no space restrictions."

"Whatever we want here, can we have it?" Sarah said.

"Not everything," said John the Great. In this world, you cannot travel in space and time. You cannot ask for gold; "But things like clothes and food and necessities do not require effort."

"We better not waste any more time," John said.

"Andreas is coming with you so you can go and get back on time," John the Great said.

"It's better that way," John said.

After saying goodbye to John the Great, they went to the room of the mind, in which Andreas told them: "All you have to do is think about where you want to go in your world and look up. Whenever you see light in the sky, close your eyes, and a few moments later you will reach that place. "It is better that you three think of one place."

"Let's all think of Sarah's house to go to the professor first to relieve him of his worries," John said. "He must not have waited for us yet and has returned." Ted and Sarah agreed.

"I'd better do it first," John said. He turned to Andreas and continued, "Where should I stand?"

Andreas pointed to the point from which they saw those words on the ground. John stood there, imagining Sarah's house on Borabora Island, staring up at the sky and seeing a light in the sky, after which a red pillar fell to the ground, and after a moment disappeared. Ted looked at Sarah and said, "It's your turn." Sarah did the same and left, then Ted and then Andreas. Moments later, all three were at Sarah's house. It was dark when they got home.

"What time was it when we went sea?" John said.

"It was morning," Ted said. It's been passed seven hours now; "It must be in the afternoon."

"Where do you think Grandpa is now?" Sarah said.

With this question of Sarah, the door was opened and a man hurried in and went to the phone. He was a professor; "Grandpa, I'm glad to see you again," Sarah said, seeing the professor.

When the professor heard that voice and saw Sarah, he suddenly fainted.

"You shouldn't have told him that," John said. He was waiting for us at sea; "We did not return and he was confronted with this scene and he was scared."

"You're right," Sarah said. And then she went to the kitchen and took the glass of water and poured it in the professor's mouth and poured some water on his face. The professor woke up and saw them and said, "What are you doing here? I have been waiting for you for several hours. No matter how hard I tried to get help from the beach patrol on the boat radio, there was no communication. It was getting dark and I was afraid I could not go back. I decided to go to the beach and ask someone for help. I turned on the boat with difficulty and was able to find my way back. I still wanted to call the beach patrol when I saw you here. Did you get here by swimming? "Didn't you think what would happen to me?"

Upon hearing the professor's words, Sarah threw herself into the professor's arms and cried, saying, "I'm sorry, Grandpa."

"Thank God you are safe," the professor said. "The rest is not important."

John and Ted also apologized to the professor. After becoming better, the professor noticed Andreas' presence and said in surprise, "Who is this gentleman?"

"His story is long," John said. You'd better take a break and we'll take a shower and then we'll tell you the story. After a short break, they told the full story to the professor. The professor was surprised of hearing that story and could not believe it. After a few minutes, the professor finally coped with the matter and said, "What do you want to do now?" "Did you bring me anything from there?"

"We came to take you there with us and to live there together," Sarah said. Of course, there are a lot of undiscovered things that could be of interest to you.

"It can be good," the professor said hesitantly.

"We do not have much time to get back there," John said. "We have to go back there in seven days. It's better to get a ticket for tomorrow and go back to New York." And he turned to Andreas and said, "Can you go back to that world from New York?" "Or do we have to come here?"

"We do not need to go back to the island," Andreas said.

"I have a little work here," Sarah said. "You better go, and then I'll join you another day in New York."

They managed at the professor's house for another three days. The next day they went to New York, and after arriving there, the professor went home with Andreas, and John and

Ted went to Ted's house. Ted's mother was overjoyed to see them again and hugged them both. After his father returned from work, Ted told them the story of another world and asked them to come with him. He said he did not want to live there without them. Ted's father was very opposed to this at first, but after John's talk, he agreed to come with them. If he did not want to live there, he could return to this world.

The next day, Sarah, John, Ted, and his family all came to the professor's house. John said to Andreas, "What must we do to return?" Is there a specific place we should go?

"We have to be in an open area where no one can cross and see us," Andreas said.

"There is a small yard behind my house where I always rest to be alone," he said. No one can disturb me there; "Because none of the surrounding houses overlook that part of the house."

"Great," said Andreas. "It's better to go there and do exactly what we did to get here."

John explained to Ted's parents and the professor how to go to another world and asked them to do the same. They went to the small yard, and Andreas said, "Because the professor and Ted's parents did not come there and did not see him, it is better to come with me."So you go first and then I will come."

After a few moments, they were all present in the palace of John the Great.

John the Great, who was already waiting for them, greeted them happily.

"As I promised, I returned before the end of the seventh day," Little John said.

"Yes," said John the Great. So in this short time left, I can talk to you about this world and the mysteries of other worlds.

John the Great asked the servants to show them their rooms. "Given the lack of time, you and I should go to a room and talk," he said to little John.

John the Great and little John went to a room and the rest went to their rooms. John the Great provided all the documents related to this world and other worlds to John.

The next day was the farewell day of John the Great. He said goodbye to the little John and the rest of the people and went to a room and the only one who could accompany him was the little John.

Little John went with him; John the Great went to a bright room with a ceiling painted with trees and lay down on a platform covered with feathers. "I'm very happy to finally be able to find you a substitution," he said. I hope that just as I discovered your world, you can also find other worlds. Then he stared at a spot on the ceiling; He clasped his hands together and then closed his eyes, and the next moment, he was no longer alive, and moments later his body disappeared.

John was just watching these scenes. After seeing these scenes, he left the room and told the others what had happened.

The next day, when everyone was at the breakfast table, John stood up and said, "My dear friends, as you know, I did not come here to live in this world; I came to discover other worlds. Yesterday I talked to John the Great and he told me the secrets of this world and gave me documents that I need your help to solve, especially Professor and Andreas. I plan to rest here for a while and then review these documents. "I want to first discover the world we live in and then look for other worlds."

"Hope for success," Ted stood up and shouted. And other people repeated the same thing out loud